MILTON C. JAMES

PRIVATE DETECTIVE

Second Revised Edition
Parts I, III and IV

Jackie Leverett

Gotham Books

30 N Gould St.
Ste. 20820, Sheridan, WY 82801
https://gothambooksinc.com/

Phone: 1 (307) 464-7800

© 2022 Jackie Leverett. All rights reserved.

No part of this book may be reproduced, stored in a retrieval system, or transmitted by any means without the written permission of the author.

Published by Gotham Books (November 30, 2022)

ISBN: 979-8-88775-152-8 (sc)

ISBN: 979-8-88775-153-5 (e)

ISBN: 979-8-88775-154-2 (h)

Because of the dynamic nature of the Internet, any web addresses or links contained in this book may have changed since publication and may no longer be valid.

The views expressed in this work are solely those of the author and do not necessarily reflect the views of the publisher, and the publisher hereby disclaims any responsibility for them.

Table of Content

PREFACE i
Chapter 1 1
  "The Long Drop Down" 1
  "Big Sam's Lie" 10
Chapter 2 16
Chapter 3 26
Chapter 4 29
Chapter 5 35
Chapter 6 38
Chapter 7 42
Chapter 8 46
Chapter 9 51
Chapter 10 56
Chapter 11 62
Chapter 12 72
Chapter 13 74
  "The Jones' is Off My List" 78

PREFACE

Growing up in the 1950s, I was fascinated by the private-eye detective stories, then only available in a single denomination, I saw on television like; "Peter Gunn", "Mannix", "77 Sunset Strip", and a bunch more later to include "The Rockford Files (James Garner)". I also liked the television series that chased and tried criminals; "The Untouchables", "Palladin", "The Defenders", "Perry Mason", "The Blue Knight (George Kennedy)", "Kojak (Telly Savalas)", and the most memorable, "Policewoman (the unconquerable Angie Dickenson)".

In the 1970's and later I really enjoyed reading Dashiell Hammett, Michael Connelly, Isaac Asimov, Louis L'Amour, Robert E. Howard, Alan Dean Foster, Charles Dickens, Frederick Douglass, Barack Obama, C.S. Forester, Alexander Kent, Douglas E. Reeman, Tony Hillerman, Andrew Lam, Van Nguyen Duong, Lam Quang Thi, Terry Brooks, Edward Rice Burroughs, Raymond Chandler, James Baldwin, Walter Mosley, Donald Goines, Langston Hughes, and many others.

My writings included screenplays and theater plays and were influenced by a lot of things. But no matter how much input I got from books (ten thousand at least), television (many years), movies (thousands), radio-dramas (hundreds), my life experiences (I am over 69 years old), or theater, it was still difficult to write a good story, even with my good imagination.

Suffice it to say that I enjoyed writing this version of my own cynical, skeptic, honest, weak, and a minority, Private-Eye operative. However, I must say that there was a scary time in my writing it where I simply lost control of the characters and <u>they</u>, indeed, were doing the writing, as I had been warned. That's ok, because the loss of control was exciting, amazing, and invigorating, and eye-opening. Now I know why a true writer, writes.

Thank you and all the best to you.

Mr. Jackie Leverett
A South Carolinian Extraordinaire\Ordinaire

This book is a rewrite of "Milton C. James—Private Detective Series, Parts 1, 2, & 3", copyright 1999". That version available as book and eBook on Amazon and elsewhere.

The rewrite involves parts one, and two. <u>Part four (IV)</u> is a brand-new story and alludes to parts of the city I grew up in. Part three, just eight pages long and dynamite, was left out because it needs a second act which I have not written, though I do have a draft in mind...somewhere.

"He who reads is a very dangerous person; shunned by dictators, feared by politicians (crooked or otherwise), loathed by slavers, avoided by the ignorant, and admired by what's left".

Chapter 1

"The Long Drop Down"
By Mr. Jackie Leverett

<u>From the Series "Milton C. James, Private Detective" (I)</u>
(c) 1999

It was high noon on a sunny Sunday. I had just come in my apartment and closed the door when I heard the click of a gun's hammer. I froze. With my keys still in my hand I locked the door from the inside. I really didn't have to do that. The door locked from the inside when I closed it, I was just fiddling around, stalling for time.

I finally turned around and there was my client's Wife, who had been missing for three months, standing nonchalant next to my dining-room table. She looked good. Damn good. Her three months missing had not hurt her at all. I had been looking for her for about a week.

The odd thing was just yesterday I read that her husband had been murdered. Well, the man had already paid me in advance. Business is business so I still had a client and work to do. Him being dead made no difference.

I had contacted Sammy the Pimp, a friend of mine and good contact on the streets and luck had it that he knew my clients' Wife. He told me." *I wouldn't be surprised if she killed him, James. You'd better watch out for that one. She's sweet, but a little messed-up in the head".* That was not surprising to hear. All my women were "sweet, but a little messed-up", these days.

All that was yesterday and for me that made her the prime suspect and here she stood in my living room in all her glory.

She had brown eyes and long brown soft hair that had to flow down to her back and who knew where else. She was almost six feet tall and wore a white dress that left most of her delicious knees exposed. She was attractive, to say the least. The picture her husband had given me didn't do her justice. She came slowly towards me.

Yes, definitely a real pretty woman, but what was wrong with this picture? Ah, yes, the gun. That was it and not just any old gun, but a silver-plated .45 that looked military issue. Damn thing much weigh a ton, not to mention being expensive, loud, and deadly. Yeah, my women were like that also…these days.

"How did you get in?" I asked casually.

She stopped, still covering me with that cannon.

"Your *doorman*, Mikee, was just getting off shift. Told him I was one of your girls. He ate that up. Brought me up in the elevator himself, the bastard, and let me in. What a gawker he is. Didn't his partner Sammy tell you that I might come see you?"

"No. Nothing was said about a call. Why would he anyhow and why would you want to see me?", I said.

I'd have to have a little talk with Mikee and Sammy, our combination doormen, security guards, pimp, etc. I knew that night was their last night on the job. Mikee had probably let her in as a joke or as a favor. Favors like this could get a guy killed.

"Sammy don't talk much", I said further. "But he did give me a line on you. He also tells me that you used to work for him. Is that true?"

"So, what if I did? What are you going to do about it? Tell my husband?" she said.

"I would if it made any sense, but he did hire me to find you. He was very upset you just disappearing like that and not calling or anything. He imagined all kinds of things had happened to you, like you fallen down a well or something", I said.

"I'll bet. How much did the bastard pay you?"

"I got $25 a day with expenses".

"What!? Is that all?"

"I couldn't squeeze anything else out of him."

"Well," she countered. "I'm not surprised. For a rich man he was even stingy with me, his beloved wife. For all he knew, I could have fell down a well a *long* time ago for all the attention he gave me. And the loneliness. I hate being lonely. He hadn't taken me out in years. So, he imagined all kinds of *bad* things had happened to me, huh? Looks like he couldn't imagine paying you a lot of money to find me", she said.

She looked to me for an answer but I didn't have anything to say.

"Even after I'd been gone for months" she said answering for me.

"You're pretty", I said. Of course, she was pretty. I was stalling again.

"How original" She replied sarcastically. "I know that".

"Know what?"

"That I'm pretty, stop deflecting. We got business", she replied.

"Lady, you and me aren't got no kind of business. What do you want?"

She started towards me again, I guess to narrow the distance between us. Her husband had been shot at very close range.

"You're tall", I said.

She looked at me blankly and said as if in a daze, "I didn't mean to be".

"You killed your husband, didn't you?"

"Yes, and I'm going to kill you too. I've already killed some of his damn pets", she replied.

"What pets?", I asked just for the fun of it.

"Margo, Sally, Millie".

"Why Millie?"

"Because she was working for Sammy and let it slip one night that she had...had him."

"Come on. You two were working the same whoredom. So, you and her were kinda in the same boat. Millie's husband used to beat her too. How could you kill a fellow sufferer?"

"Easy!", she screamed. "I-don't-share! Get that right in your head and maybe I won't shoot your head off!".

"Well, they both usually take care of themselves. I don't get the notion of why you were jealous of a pimp. I mean, every one of his whores was probably sleeping with him. It's kind of a duty, like employee relations, you could say. So, you've killed four people. Isn't time to stop? You're going to get the electric chair, I mean, you get the chair for just one. You nailed four. Looks like overkill to me, Sister."

As I talked, I was edging toward her as fast as I dared. I managed a few feet before she smiled and extended her cannon in warning.

She had noticed my shuffle.

"I ain't *your* Sister! Overkill, my ass. I'd do it all over again. You don't know what's been going on in my life. You don't know how bad he treated me.

Did he tell you that he would bring women to our apartment while I was there? Did he tell you that he got sicker and sicker and eventually made me *watch* as he made love to them? No? Well, think about that Mr. Know-it-all-Detective. No jury in this world would send me to the chair for killing him and his bitches! They'll give me a medal!"

She stopped talking and looked around. As if she heard something.

"I doubt they'll give you a medal", I said.

"Give me a smoke", she answered.

"I quit a long time ago, smoking's not good for your health. Tell me, why did you kill his dog? I thought that extreme. A dead man lying in a pool of blood and right next to him his dog."

"I hate dogs", she said. It was his damn dog, but who do you think got up early in the damn morning to walk damn thing? Me! Me! Me! But if he had got any other kind of dog, it would have been…. alright".

"Something other than a dachshund?", I asked.

"Yeah".
"So, you killed the dog simply because it was your husband's, and by killing her she represented your husband, so you got the pleasure of killing your husband twice"?

"Good Grief! You know, Sammy told me you were smart but what book you been reading? I killed the dog because she wasn't a husky and male. I especially love blue-eyed huskies. You can understand that can't you?"

"Oh," I said. "So, you shot her?"

"You got that right, one bullet. I wasn't going waste gun on that dumb bitch."

"Looks like your husband loved bitches", I said looking down.

"What?"

"Nothing. Did he keep fish?"

"No. Why you ask that?" she said.

"Oh, just a question".

Her eyes went hard. "Don't get cute. Sammy warned you to stay away. But no, you had to keep snooping. You want to put me in jail. I know I wouldn't like jail. For that I gotta kill you, Mr. James."

"Yes, you said that already. But I have to ask you why. I'm not one of your husband's pets."

I could see she was considering this. She lowered her eyes and the left arm holding the gun. I managed another shuffle and then a full step. First her eyes then her arm came up. Either she was too alert or I too cautious. We stared at each other. Her brown eyes against my brown eyes.

What did she see in mine? Fear? You bet she did.

Fear was on me like sand on a beach from my first sight of the gun. I'd never been shot before and I wanted to keep the losing streak going.

There was no fear in her eyes though, no fear at all but something was there. I concentrated more and still saw nothing. No hate. No malice, yet she stood there not two feet away ready to shoot me.

Then I saw what I was looking for. She had no feelings.

"Isn't that too much gun for your little hand?" Her hands were not little. "Did you shoot him with that?"

"No. This is my...Lover. I bought it. It's a part of me.", she said.

She looked down, bought up her right hand and slowly stroked the gun's top, length-wise, and then its sides lovingly.

"I'd never shoot him with *this*", she purred looking up at me. "What a disgusting thought. I used a cheap .38 that I dumped later. He was dead, I think, after my third shot. The last two were just for fun".

I swallowed as lightly as I could. It seemed to take a long time and all the while, as she stroked that gun, she watched me. Her eyes were now alive. I could see something in them.

I could see that Mrs. Lurleenie Angelique Garvin had somehow, somewhere, lost it.

One didn't have to be no doctor to see it in her actions. Her husband had abused her mind and probably her body for a long time. He had paid the ultimate price, but even that did not help her and ultimately left her alone to suffer forever.

Abruptly she stopped stroking the gun as if I had caught her doing something obscene.

She took deliberate aim at my chest. We were so close that she could not extend her arm.

Well, this is it, I thought. The end of my dreams and a not so illustrious life. But Hell, it was illustrious to *me*, dammit! I beamed a smile at Lurleenie. She returned my smile with bewilderment and anger.

Then I started to laugh. It was a long laugh, an "I don't give a damn if you shoot me" laugh. It was a lie.

Her gun-hand started to shake but I didn't care. She squinted her eyes as if she was looking into the sun and covered the distance between us. She put the gun gently to my belly. We played the eye tag game again, but now I noticed that her eyes had turned black. I blinked and looked again. They were still black.

She reached around my waist with her free hand and moved it up to my middle back, pulling me gently to her. Her lips parted, covering mine and her tongue forced its way through my teeth, playing with the roof of my mouth.

"Angelique", I muttered with a shudder.

She took her cold lips from mine and backed a step. Lowering the gun, she took it with her right hand and handed it to me butt first.

I came toward her with the gun at my side has she backed away. Something came over me. I wanted this woman in my arms, to comfort her, to subdue her till I could call the Police...well, maybe *not* call the Police. Maybe I'd just keep her. She probably could beat the murder rap. After all, she probably was insane.

She could get off with an insanity plea, be committed, and I could visit her, and after a few years we could get together and...

"Now, who's crazy!?", she said aloud, her eyes going wide with pleasure. She had read my thoughts. She didn't want me though.

She slowly raised her right arm and the palm came up just as slowly, her way of wanting me to stay where I was. She was backing up again.
I followed her anyway, uncomprehending.

She backed to the sliding door leading to the balcony, reached behind her, touched the latch and slide it open. I followed her to the sliding door and by the time I got there she had backed to the balcony's wall.

We stared again at each other, me silently pleading, begging her to stop.

She blinked her eyes but not from nervousness; her body was oddly relaxed, her hands hung lightly at her sides, shoulders down, resigned.

She put one leg over the balcony, straddling the wall. I came forward. She turned her now brown eyes to look at me, shook her head. This was what she wanted. I could stop her, but I knew she wanted me and the world to just leave her alone.

She looked down over the wall to the street below and then there was a banging commotion at my door. I could hear Detective Lieutenant Harvey Miller screaming "Ok, James we know you're in there! We want the dame! Open up or we'll knock it down!"

She heard them too, looking back at me triumph and defiance in her eyes.

The Police finally crashed through the door. Old Harv and four uniformed-officers barging through to my living room, taking in the whole scene.

The all had their guns out, for all the damn good it would do.

She smiled, at them, winked at me, closed her eyes and with no hesitation or sound she took herself sideways and backwards over the balcony.

We were 19 stories straight up.

The End

"Big Sam's Lie"
By Mr. Jackie Leverett

From the Series "Milton C. James, Private Detective (II)
(C) 1999

Me and my shadow sat in my new office, at my old wooden desk, in my old wooden chair. One side of my face was nestled in my right palm. I was looking at the walls. I'd have to do something about those walls, I thought. Maybe hang some pictures or put up some lovely wallpaper. Maybe buy some new chairs for the waiting room. My clients would like that, they'd have a nice place to put their feet on the floor. Be good for business and...

Wait a minute, I thought. I don't have a waiting room.

Maybe I needed a bigger office. Some clients would be nice too.

Maybe I shouldn't move here in the first place, but I really didn't have a choice at the time.

When Mrs. Lurleenie Angelique Garvin jumped to her death from my apartment, thus solving my last case, it effectively put me out of a home and an office. A home because I couldn't stand to stay there anymore and relive her committing suicide by putting herself gracefully over my balcony to the street, nineteen-stories below. She landed on top of a car. I needed a new office because her Husband hired me there to find her. I didn't do a good job. She found me.

The office I had now was my third in less than a year, and that move came about when my then Landlord began to make overtures. Overtures like in exchange for free rent she'd expect me to do certain things that didn't involve maintenance in the apartments...

Still, she didn't look that bad. Maybe I should have taken her up on the offer. *I mean, a guy doesn't get that many really good offers these days, anyway...*

Before I could finish the thought my front-door, behind me, opened. *Damn*, I thought, I'd forgotten to turn the darn desk around.

I turned me and my chair around. The first person I saw was 6-feet tall and had to weigh one-hundred-eighty pounds. He could have played a football linebacker. The next one came in and closed the door behind him. He was 6-feet '4" and wider. They both wore opened long black coats that covered dark grey suits with white shirt and green tie. Their shoes were black and highly shined.

The six-footer came to my desk and the other guy stood by my door as if guarding it. I knew they were crooks.

"What can I do for you guys", I chirped.

The six-footer leaned forward answered me in a monotonic but distinctly female voice.

"I'm not a *guy*, Mister!" she said. "Name's Margo!".

"Oh! Sorry", I said. "Could a fooled me", I added under my breath and revised her weight downward.

The other guy came up alongside his partner. I guessed they came as a set. They had me helmed in real neat. I felt like a small tug boat getting ready to duck two big ships.

"Call me Earl. You James?", he asked.

"As far as I know. Milton C. James, at your service. My friends call me Jessie", I said.

"Why that?", asked Margo.

I didn't feel like explaining, so I said "Oh, just a joke" She still didn't get it.

I got a bit of anxious energy but I couldn't fight them. My gun, the one that shoots, was behind me in my desk. It would take a lot to get it, and the way these two were watching me, I had no chance.

The guy, Earl, seemed to read my mind was about to laugh but checked and just smiled knowingly. The girl studied me with interest. I studied her back and thought she was kinda cute.

"Horse manure", said my inner voice. "To you, all girls are cute".

I ignored the voice and studied the girl intently. I started to feel Old Man Lust, that demon that seems to be in all us poor men, whisper in my ear. This Margo sweetie was like an Amazon in a grey suit. I liked Amazons, any way I could get them. They could come anytime if they were not too rough. She looked good, but the extra bulge near her left breast gave me pause. I must have got to her because her face flushed as if she could read my mind. A fascinating red flush started at her cheeks and went down to her neck to where her shirt collar shirt stopped it.

For all I knew the flush went further.

I noticed that Earl watched her also, with that certain interest only men thought they possessed. This was not the way us tough guys were supposed to act, openly lusting after a female, but he enjoyed the show as much as I did.

Margo closed her eyes and shook her head.

You can't shake that off honey, I thought.

"Like I said guy and doll, what do you want"?

Margo said, "Big Sam wants to see ya."

My mouth went dry, my right eyelid twitched once, twice, stopped. I tried to laugh bravely but all that came out was a sick, jerky chuckle that wouldn't spook a rabbit. My left elbow jerked once on its own volition. I could hear my own heartbeat. Hell, I couldn't even swallow.

With false bravado I tried to summon up my tough guy act but could only manage a strained reply.

"Big Sam. Big Sam? Why! What on earth would *he* want with me! I'm a pretty straight, law-abiding guy!" I said.

"Maybe that's why he wants to see ya", Earl said as he moved to a window, pulled the curtains back and stared out.

"Maybe you boys should take a hike", I said. "I got real business to attend to. The doors behind you", I said as I swiveled my chair around to my desk, presenting my back to them. I began shuffling papers with a nonchalance I really didn't fee.

Then there was a click. Then another and another. I knew exactly what it was; someone playing with the hammer of a piston. Pulling it back and letting it fall on an empty chamber. I hoped that all the rest of those damn chambers were just as empty as the first three.

I turned around slowly to see Margo looking straight at me while she played with the pistol at her side.

The safety has to be on, I thought. I knew I wouldn't try that trick without it being on. At least I hoped it was on. You could shoot your foot off or something if it wasn't.

"I'm listening. I don't think I heard you right, Mr. James", Margo said as she pulled the hammer back. There was another *click* as the it locked.

"Look", Earl said talking to the window pane. "Don't get riled,

James. We got orders to bring youse in. Orders are orders. How we do it is like up to us. But I'll tell you this"

He turned from the window and looked straight at me. "We could do it hard way or we could do the job easy. I don't give a cat's ass which."

"I don't either", Margo said with a voice that was sounding better all the time.

"Well, what does he want?", I asked, frustration rising.

"How the hell should I know, Mr.-Know-it-All Detective!", Earl replied.

"And what if I don't feel like going with you? What guarantee do I have that this is not just some fancy way to bump me off? I got enemies", I said

Margo's answer was to reach in her coat pocket, pulling out a short black object that she screwed into the muzzle of her pistol. She aimed it at me and pulled the trigger. There was a metallic click when the hammer hit a dry chamber.

I blinked, tried to look unconcerned, failed. She'd had darn near scared me to death with that stunt.

"I always keep the first five chambers empty. The safety's broke", she said with big grin.

Earl said, "If'n we were sent to kill ya, you'd be dead already, see? Get a coat and let's blow. Ain't polite to keep the boss waitin!".

"Okay, okay", I said and got up and went to my plain wooden coat rack and put on my hat and coat. I started for the door. The guy and the doll followed.

I opened my second-floor office door, waited for both of them

to come out and locked it. With Margo in front, myself in the middle and Earl in back, we went down the white marbled and mahogany railed stairs. About half way down, the door to the street opened and in stepped Sammy "The Pimp" Paul. He started up the stairs, looked up and saw us coming down and stopped.
I could see his concern. Something about the procession set off alarms but when we got to him, he just said, "James! Man, I need to talk to you. I got big trouble!".

"Sorry, got a job, Brother. Stop by tomorrow", I said.

"What time?", he replied, blocking our way.

We stopped. "Never mind", I said trying hard not to mention his name. "I'll call you".

"How the Hell are you gonna call *me* if I'm on the streets?", he said trying hard to look over Margo's head to me.

"Get a phone", Margo said as she gently pushed Sammy out of the way. I looked at him and he just kind of laughed as we went by. "Don't rough him up too bad, boys. I need him", Sammy said.

No one answered him.

Outside they hustled me along the street to the next block where the standard issue limo waited patiently like a black bug. We all got in like one big happy family, myself in the back seat with Earl as Margo drove. I was relieved to see that there was no third person in the back seat.

These limos made me very nervous with their famous *one-way rides*. But, like Earl said, if they had come to kill me...

Big Sam's place was a good hour out of town. Earl turned to watch me. I watched him back and snorted. *What the heck*, I thought. I relaxed, closed my eyes and tried to nap.

Chapter 2

The next thing I knew someone was shoving me awake. I did more than nap. That ought to have impressed them.

"You snore", Margo said.

I smiled and winked at her. She ignored me. We were parked in front of a house. I got out and saw it was a spooky looking number with that abandoned look.

Since it was rainy, dreary, and dark, the spookiness was even more enhanced. Black rain-soaked stone glared gloomily at us though moonlight that I had not noticed before. The house had a huge black, metal studded door with a large metal ring in the middle with a huge metal square itching to pound. Use that knocker and everyone in the house would know that someone was calling.

Surprisingly, we did not go in through that door but went around to the right side of the house and immediately a plain white door with no keyhole. There must have been a button or something to open it because Margo reached up and used three fingers to press something. With an angry hiss the door opened and we entered a long hall, walls and ceiling black. I guess the hallway was carpeted because the walk was soft, the floor dark, the lighting poor.

At the end of the hall was a wall, but Margo walked up to it and I thought for a second that she was going to walk in to it. The wall opened like a regular door and Margo stepped in and held it open for us. Here I hesitated.

All this darkness was just too much for me. They must have either practiced this entrance to put fear in the person they were bringing in or the entrance was just way it was. Whatever. If meant to intimidate, all it accomplished was to tick my temper.

Earl pushed me into the room. Margo helped by grabbing my coat lapel and pulled me further in into Big Sam's office, closing the door.

We were in a large room with the typically large collection of books, on all three walls, that had been read or were intended to be read later, or there just to impress. A lot of them seemed to have been read because, as best as I could see, they were not dusty. The shelves were white and the books were bound in black.

Three chandlers hung in perfect alignment and distance from each other on the ceiling. Only the first and third one was lit and just half-lighted. The one in the middle could barely be discerned.

Again, the spooky effect but this time it didn't mess with my temper. Such sameness in craziness, may again just be the way things really were. Maybe all this was not a show.

At the back of the room, facing out of the wall, were more shelves of books to the ceiling. Behind was a large mahogany desk that we approached.

I was startled when a book snapped shut, and a section of a bookshelf in front of me turned and looked at me. Someone had been standing with their back to me as I entered. Someone dressed in the black reading a book, just in front of the desk. A white face looked at me serenely with light-green eyes and light-green mascara and plain white lips.

The stare was steady, unblinking like a cat.

"Turn on the light", she said in a deep masculine voice.

Margo turned to flick a wall switch that switched on the desk light. That light revealed a tall, mature woman with a fine older woman's figure standing in front of the desk.

Wow, I thought.

She turned away from us and seemed to glide to the desk, came around a dark chair and sat down. "Good evening, Mr. James. I hope my boys were not *too* rough on you. I'm Big Sam".

I stared at her. My mouth dropped. I didn't believe it. My hand went to my heart, but went to the wrong side. I looked at Margo and saw her smirk.

Earl also looked smug with that "*you don't know nothing, Jack*" look on his face.

"Yeah? And I'm Cinderella!", I finally said back to this Big Sam.

I could sense Margo and Earl move toward me. But Big Sam just laughed and raised her hand for them to stop.

"It's alright, boys" Are you really surprised that the most feared gangster in town is a woman? I'm very disappointed in you, Mr. James. My people told me you were more intelligent, more sophisticated than that!".

"Sure, I'm smart", I rasped back after swallowing nothing. "But even I can be surprised. Are you really Big Sam or is this some kind of joke?"

She reached in to a drawer and pulled out a .38 caliber pistol.

While she held it on me, she reached in to another drawer and pulled out a 22. caliber pistol. She held them both up for me to see.

"Do *these* looks like I'm joking?"

"No, Mam!", I said chokingly. I had inside information that Big Sam's victims, her hits, were riddled with .38 and .22 caliber bullets. It gave the Police fits. I looked at Earl and Margo.

Could it be that they were responsible for all those murders?

"Cut the "Mam" stuff and sit on it", she said and laid both guns on the desk.

I sat in a simple black wooden high-backed chair with no arm rests. Margo moved to stand behind me. She moved quiet for someone so large, but I could smell her perfume. Her wonderful, wonderful perfume...

"I got a job for you." Big Sam said.

"No. No, you don't lady. I don't work on your side of the law."

"Take it easy, Big Boy, the jobs legit. There's someone I want you to find", she said reaching in to the middle drawer. I expected her to pull out another gun, or a bazooka or some such other nonsense, but was surprised when she pulled out a wallet-sized picture and shoved it to me.

"I want you to find her for me", Big Sam said.

I leaned forwarded, looked at the picture and said, "Find who?"

She just sat there and gave me a hostile look and said, "Her! Damn you! Her!". She looked down and saw that the picture was white-side up and groaned "Oh, damn!" and flipped it over.

Margo said, "Looks like you pretty smart after all, Mr. D-tect-tive", Margo said.

"Shut-up!", Big Sam told her. Margo shut-up.

I took a good gander at the full-length color picture and saw a good looking, but not pretty girl in her mid-twenties, with hip length red hair and brown eyes.

Her eyebrows were black, which was a dead giveaway that her hair was colored. The eyes were intense and had a defiant and mesmerizing quality. There was also hostility, a deep hostility because of…what? Having been hurt? Abused?

"She got eyes that could kill", I finally said to no one in particular.

"You got that wrong, she wouldn't hurt a damn fly," Big Sam said. "That picture was taken at a bad time. There was something that I didn't want her to have and she just threw a tantrum. Incredible that someone so old could be so childish".

"Age is no guarantee of maturity", I replied.

"Don't go *Freud* on us Mister!", Margo said.

"Now Margo, let Mr. James have his way. This time", Big Sam said.

"Okay, you want me to find your daughter", I said.

Margo snickered but stopped when Big Sam gave her a scowl.

"And why don't you call the police or use some of your boys?", I said, throwing my thumb back at Margo and Earl.

Big Sam stood up and walked to a window and pulled the black drapes open. It was dark and the rain came down hard.

"Damn, this weather is getting on my nerves", she said. Closing the drapes, she came languidly over to me and sat on the edge of the desk. She leaned close to my face.

"Oh, don't be so dumb! Get real! The police must not, I repeat, must not find out about Marie. Missing or otherwise. *And,* if I try to use my boys to find her, I run the risk of my enemies finding out. They'd use her against me".

Slowly, languidly, she crossed her legs. The black long dress she wore was slit up the side, giving me a glimpse of Heaven and Hell.

As I looked up toward her face, my eyes were also greeted by a pair of magnificent...

A-ha! I thought to myself. She's trying a typical female trick. Her languid, almost careless motions were the give-away. She was using her femalese on me. The worse thing was that it was working.

I cleared my throat and said, "I'll find her, Big Sam".

After seeing those legs, I would have promised her anything.

"My fee for big crooks is one-hundred a day, plus expenses", I said

"Very funny. Make it one-hundred-fifty a day, but you got two weeks to do it".

"Two weeks!", I cried. "Lady, I might not find her in two months!"

"Oh, you expected to stick me with your fees for two months? *That* don't sound very honest, Mister Jones!", spreading her arms.

"Don't get excited, don't get excited. After just a week I would have come in to negotiate a lower price. In any case you'd get an itemized bill, I don't gouge anybody. If your sources were any good, they would have told you that too", I said.

The room went silent as Big Sam glowering down at me. I turned in my chair to Margo and saw her hand in her upper coat pocket, as was Earl with the same posture behind her. He didn't have to do nothing. He had the easiest job. The two women could shoot me front and back with bullet holes.

The tension eased when Big Sam lowered her arms.

I tried to get some comfort out of my chair. "Tell me where you saw her last".

"Here, in this house", Big Sam said.

"How long ago"?

"How long ago, *please"*, Margo interrupted.

I turned my head and said, "Normally I don't mix with the hired help, but you're starting to get on my nerves, *please". Now be quiet and let a man work!*

"You weaselly Son of a Bitch!", Margo said. I heard her step and thought that this was it. I didn't dare look back.

"Stop it! Out!", Big Sam said.

"But..."

"No buts, Margo! Out!"

Margo left, but didn't slam the door.

"The last time I saw here her was two years ago", Big Sam said.

"*Two* years!", I said.

"Yeah, two years", said Earl. "You hard of hearing or what?"

I didn't reply. No sense in pushing my luck.

Big Sam said, "No farewell letter, no call, nothing. She didn't even pack. All her stuff is still in her room. Find her...please.", Big Sam said.

"I'll find her", I said, "But it's gonna take some time. The trail is cold. She could be anywhere; I'll have to start from scratch. Two years. Damn. But I can understand you worrying. If I had a daughter who took off like that, I'd be worried to.

Anything could happen to her. You'd not know how she was doing, if's she's in trouble, or where she is..."

"Oh, I know exactly where she is", interrupted Big Sam.

I thought I was hearing wrong. "What?!"

"I know where she is. I got sources and they came through last week", Big Sam said smoothly.

If I had a gun, I would have shot her right then and there.

"Sam, or Big, or whatever the Hell your name is", I screamed. "If you know where she is, why don't you just go and get her and stop wasting my time and scaring me half to death!?"

She got up from the edge of the desk, pushing herself close to me, went around her desk and sat down.

She lowered her head and brought up both hands to her face. I got suspicious; couldn't figure out if she was on the level or was this another female trick. She raised her head and looked at me. There were tears. Maybe it wasn't a trick.

"Because I know she wouldn't come with me and where she's at...I would have to strong arm my way in", she said.

"Can't be done then", I replied off handedly.

"You're a smart guy, James. You'll figure out a way", she said.

"Can't be done", I repeated.

"Two-hundred-fifty a day and...*your life!*", she said a serious glare. Tears and all she meant business.

"In that case I'll figure out a way, but one more thing".

"*What* one more thing?", Earl said gruffly.

I ignored him. "Is Margo married?", I said to Big Sam. "I mean, er, does she have a boyfriend? Could you like fix me up with her?", I said like a beggar walking a fish-line over a crevasse.

They both laughed, and Big Sam said, "Margo's a grown woman and goes with whoever and whatever she pleases. Best you forget her though, James. She might kill you just for the fun of it. Besides, anyone could see she don't like you", Big Sam said.

"Ok, ok", I managed.

Sam reached under her desk and Margo came in. She also reached in the middle drawer and pulled out wad of money and tossed it to me. I caught it.

"There's thirteen-hundred there."

"Er, I don't give refunds.", I said, but actually did not like the number thirteen.

"And I don't do receipts, smart guy", Big Sam said. "Margo will tell you all you need to know. You got two weeks. Get on it. Take him out the front door boys."

"The front door?!", Margo and Earl said in unison.

Big Sam shook her head as if to clear it "I must be losing my mind.

The back-door boys, I meant the *back* door."

I stood there taking in this "door" business. It didn't matter to me which door I went out, just so I got out of there. I gave Big Sam one more look. She gave me one more look. I got up and turned away from her and walked the way I came in. She turned her desk light off. Darkness was back. I kept my walk as normal as I could and heard Margo and Earl behind me. We went out of the presence of Big Sam, murderer, racketeer, embezzler, high-thief, Madam, most feared gangster in town, and all in all, a real good-looking woman, and a Mother.

Chapter 3

We three adults managed to go out the same door we came in, which I guess was the back door, and were now in the limo on the way back to my office. I sat alone in the back. I looked out my window at the dark and the rain.

"Lucky you!", Margo said, turning sideways in the front-seat and throwing her cute mouth at me, "Good thing we asked about the door. There might have had a t-t-terrible miscommunication. When Big Sam says *"Take em out the front door"* it means we ice kill em! *Lucky* you".

"Would've been an awful shame", Earl said while driving.

"Yeah", I replied. "I'm a real lucky guy. So, where is she?", I asked Margo.

"Where's who?", Margo replied.

"Come on, give me a break. I'm on your side now. I don't want to fight". I leaned forward, "I got other, more friendly things in mind".

"I don't give a goat's-ass damn what you got in mine. I got half a mind to drill ya where you ya sit". She turned back around.

"Just *half*, Margo? I'm glad to hear that. There may be hope for me and you after all. Besides, Big Sam wouldn't be too pleased with you putting holes in me before I find her wayward daughter."

Earl looked up a me through the rear-view mirror.

"Stop riding her, friend. She got a temper, so back off", he clipped.

I must have been feeling cocky, why I don't know, because I

replied, "Who's this, Margo? Your boyfriend?".

Earl pushed hard on the breaks and I nearly came over the front seat as the car's back-end started skidding out of control on the wet road. He neatly brought the car under control and we pulled over. Earl killed the motor.

They both took off their hats and turned to stare at me. It was clear in their faces, especially their angry eyes, that I had crossed a line, uttered a taboo.

I spoke up, "I'm sorry Margo, Earl. I don't know what got in me. Must be the weather and having been muscled around the whole time. I get impatient some time and..."

They turned and looked at each other for a long moment, communicating silently only as murderers can. Margo shook her head slowly. Earl groaned and looked out his window.

I sat still and knew this time to keep quiet, but a small voice in me wanted to tell them both the drop dead. Just to see what they would do. Reason won out and I kept my mouth shut.

Finally, Margo said, "Drive".

With a crazy slowness, as if it was his last protest left, Earl reached up for the key, turned it and the motor sprang. I let out a breath of relief that was unnaturally loud in the car.

Sitting back, I could feel my leg muscles relax. Earl pulled back on the road and for five minutes nobody said anything.

Margo brooded for five minutes and when they were up, as if on que, she said to the windshield, "Marie is in a Nunnery about 100 miles from here. Since you're so darn smart *and* a de-tecttive to boot, you should have no trouble finding her! Stop the damn car!", she said.

We stopped. Earl turned and threw a smile at me that was not a smile at all.

"Get out!", Margo said.

I quickly got out of the car and watched them drive away, as the rain took advantage of came down harder.

I walked along in the rain feeling sorry for myself. But my self-pity didn't last long. I stopped, raised my head and shouted in the direction they went, *"A nunnery! What the hell is she doing in a nunnery?"* The answer was two loud thunderbolts across the sky, shaped like hands, followed by three crashes that shook me to my bones. I wanted to say "sorry" but was too scared for the moment to even breath.

The lights of the car were gone, the rain decided to come down harder, and I had to content myself with silently cussing a woman I had never seen to include Big Sam, Earl, and sexy Margo. I went easy on Margo.

Chapter 4

A burly, one-eyed, female truck driver from Wisconsin, in blue jeans and the worse checkered shirt I ever saw, stopped and gave me a lift. She darns near talked my head off about politics and everything else while I politely, gentlemanlike, listened.

Fortunately, she couldn't take me all the way home so I had to walk the last couple miles in the rain. The rain came down then so hard I thought I'd drown standing up. I got home in the early morning, just in time to catch a radio report that said we were having the worst rainstorm in twenty years. I believed it. But what the heck, in a way I liked the thunder and the sheets of rain. It cleansed the soul somehow. In a way it was like being on the beach, only wet.

I had these crazy thoughts as I sloughed in my kitchen, my feet quesh queshing all the way, full of water. I wanted something hot, even if it meant coffee. I got water from the tap into the old perk and was pouring what I thought was coffee from a can I got from the refrigerator's top. I stopped in mid-pour.

I heard footsteps. Someone was in my apartment my apartment!

I put the coffee can down and reached up slowly to the top of the refrigerator.

"Leave it!", grumbled a short unfriendly but familiar voice.

I slowly raised my hands.

"Get it, Lefty!", came the next order.

Someone came up behind me and reached the top of the refrigerator with his right hand.

I looked him in the face and said, "Why do you people have

names like "Lefty" but you do everything with your right hand? Damn peculiar", I said with a croak.

He frowned at me for a moment and said, "I don't have to answer your damn questions".

"He's right", said the voice. "We ask the questions here. Police, James. Put your hands down".

I turned around and there stood Detective Lieutenant Harvey Miller. Old "Hard Core Harv" they called him at the station. They also called him Chief, Organized Crime Division. He was dressed in plain, rather bland, clothes. He was accompanied by two police officers. Lefty, a short stocky fellow with a fast-retreating hair line was also in plain clothes.

Wonderful, I thought. *More trouble.* Harvey was examining the pistol Lefty gave him. It was a heavy, silver-plated 45.

"Damn strange looking gun for a working guy", Harvey said. "Didn't take you for the spiffy type, James."

The coppers laughed of course.

"I didn't buy it. It was, er, sort of given to me. It won't shoot. If you look closely, you'll see cement in the barrel".

Harvey looked. "Ah, that's wonderful." He tossed me the gun. I caught it and carefully put it back in the cabinet.

"How you expect to stop anybody with a gun that won't shoot?", Harvey observed.

"I'd hit em over the head with it".

"Smart", Harvey replied.

"Thank you", I said graciously.

"Thank you, my ass", he said. "Let's get to business.

We heard you took a nice little ride tonight, Mr. James. A ride to Big Sam's".

He walked to me, looking me up and down. "I'm surprised you in one piece. I don't see no bullet holes in you, so what did you guys talk about?"

"Oh, this and that", I said and turned to finish making the coffee". "You know. Stuff like the weather, Christmas lists, and you know I can't talk to you about a client. It's against the rules."

"Oh, yea? Whose rules?", Lefty said.

"My profession's rules and you know them too. We detectives are professionals. Highly trained, like you guys", I said.

"Hey, you trying to get funny with me!", Lefty said.

"Wouldn't try it", I said turning to face them.

Harvey said, "Don't go talking that client crap to me or do you want to take another ride, this time downtown?!"

"You got a lotta nerve, coming in my house Willy Nillie! I bet you don't even get a search warrant. Get out, all of you, damn you. Get out before I call the cops!"

"Dumb shit, we *are* the cops. I got probable cause!", Harvey said, his fists balled at his side.

I said, "You got *probable* nothing and I don't give a damn what you got. Get out you, dumb-ass cop!"

Harvey hit me. I was on the floor when they grabbed him as he attempted to kick my ribs.

Lefty was shocked. "Why did you do that, Lieutenant? Come on, lets got out of here".

"Alright, alright!", said Harvey as he struggled from the other two. "All of you go to the car. It'll be ok. I'll be right there".

"You shouldn't hit him again, Lieutenant. It's against the law you know", replied Lefty.

Harvey stared at him and Lefty said, "Ok, Ok. We'll be outside but don't take too long, *Sir*".

I nodded to Lefty with a new respect. He nodded back and all three men left. We heard their footsteps receding and presently the opening and slamming of car doors.

For a few moments we just stared at other and I said, "Did you have to hit me, Harv?"

"Did you have to call me dumb-ass? And don't call me *Harv*! You know I hate that name. Had to make it look good, didn't I? Actually, I gave you a light hit anyway and you know it. What you got?"

The coffee had stopped perking and I poured a cup.

"You call that "light"! Whatever. Well, *Harvey*, for your information Big Sam's daughter's is missing. She wants me to find her". I grinned. "She doesn't trust your coppers. I wonder why?".

"Very funny and what do you mean by *she*? You take the case?"

"I'm broke and the *she* is a dame, Harvey. A dame that gave me no choice anyway, *and* I got offered a lot of money".

"A woman! Big Sam! Ha! Now I know you crazy!"

"It's true!"

"Someone's pulling your leg buddy. Big Sam's a guy."

"Got any proof of that?", I asked.

"I don't need no proof. Sam's a guy's name. Besides, no self-respecting hood would take orders from a dame. It just ain't natural."

"See", I said pointing a finger. "That ain't proof, that's just sexism. Think about it Harv. You all got any pictures of Big Sam?"

Harvey didn't answer.

No!", I said. "I know you don't. Has anybody actually seen him? No! All we do is hear about the murders, the business, the rackets he runs. So, my friend the *he* could be a she", I said.

"You're nuts", Harvey replied grinning. "I still say someone's puttin one over on ya. Big Sam a woman, ha! That's a good one. What other little jewels did you dig up?"

"Go fish", I said. "I already told you too much. Leave me at least the facade of client privilege."

He held up both his hands, shaking them palm out and said "Oh I'm always impressed by big words!". He put both hands down and got serious.

"Listen, James. One day I'm gonna put that bastard, bitch, or whatever behind bars and throw away the damn key!"

"Great. I know you will, one-day, but in the meantime, lay off a bit while I work the case. I gotta eat and pay rent Harv. I'll be in touch".

"Ok, you got it. What do we do for the big finally?"

"Hell", I said. "I'm not going to let you hit me again. Just leave with a scowl. I'm still paying for this furniture here.

"Ok, but one little jewel from me before I go".

"Oh? What's that?"

"Big Sam's *is* a guy and we know for sure *he* ain't got no daughter." He laughed all the way to my front-door and slammed it hard on the way out.

I just stood there, stunned, and drank my funny tasting coffee that turned out to be tea.

Chapter 5

The next morning, I packed my other gun, the *.32 Colt* that shoots, and hopped in my car. There was only one nunnery in the whole state. *Funny, I thought, there should be more nunneries, it ain't as if we don't have the virgins...*

Just about the whole drive up I thought about Harvey's bombshell---"Big Sam ain't got no daughter".

If that was true then what was I doing? I felt my right breast. There, nestled warm and cozy, was three-hundred bucks for fun and expenses, the rest safely hidden away at home. Money explains just about everything and my confusion went away. About three hours later the road I was on started winding up to a hill and on that hill stood the nunnery.

Ah, nunnery. Seems like most of the women I dated these days acted like they lived there. Whatever. I drove in and parked on pretty white stones the size of marbles. My car was the only one there but that did not surprise me. One could see the building while driving up too it. It was not very inviting. I turned off the motor and was greeted by an even louder silence. The three-story building, black and grey stoned, demanded attention.

The building was huge and didn't even look like a nunnery but more like a pillbox bunker, crescent shaped like a helmet. It was a two-hundred feet wide, two-hundred deep, three-stored architecture. For all its height it had only three windows on the first floor, two on the second, and one on the third. As I sat in my car I had the odd feeling that the building looked back at me. That was when I snapped my fingers, understanding why. The foundation must have been bad because the building seemed to be leaning toward me as if to stare me down.

I got out of my car and walked across the yard. *The white stones were probably there to give the place at least some light,* I thought. As I crunched over the rocks, I noted that the only sound around was my crunching steps. *The more to hear you with*, I thought and stopped. No bird sung or even flew by. No cricket cricketed, no bees hummed, no butterfly fluttered. Even the tall trees behind the building did not stir as if not to dare. *But no wonder*, I thought, there was no wind.

To my left there was a small lake with deep forest behind it. The lake was smooth as glass and the stones stopped well before it. I studied that placid lake for a while. No fish jumped. I didn't like that. Heck, at least one fish should be jumping and giving its fin to the world. Life in the deep couldn't be all that nice.

A wind finally moved over the lake's surface but even that seemed to say, "*don't stare, move on*".

To my right about one-hundred yards there stood another forest of tall trees, all standing too close together as if to defend each other against something. The small white stones went right up that tree line. At least on that side, if something came out of the woods, it would be outlined against the whiteness of the small stones and the blackness of the trees. The lake offered some security also. It didn't look very inviting to swim in.

I got the feeling that somebody wanted to know, at all times, when the building was being approached. If that was the case I was being watched right now.

I started again toward the building and thought again that somebody didn't like visitors. But at a nunnery? How many bad people visit a nunnery?

I stopped again. *Well,* I thought, *I'm bad*, but I was not going to flatter myself that all this security was for dangerous me. I absently felt my left breast. It was good to feel *Norma Jean*, my silver-plated 45…but no, *Norma* was at home. What I felt was my .32 pistol, the one that shoots. That made me feel better.

I walked up to a front-door, if you could call it that, that any bank would be proud of. It was solid metal and painted black. I noted a large, round knocker a foot across.

I used it twice to announce my presence. Silence greeted me. I was about to knock again when it started to open. First there was an almost silent *swoosh* as if the door was glad to exhale. Then it opened in oiled silence. I pushed it and met very little resistance. A large man in a ridiculously tight white suit met me.

"May I help you, Sir?", he said in growling monotonic voice.

I looked him up and down and said, "You don't look like a monk. I want to speak with the Mother Superior, please".

"Well, Mr. James", he replied as he came closer. "I'm the *Mother!*" He grabbed my shirt with both hands, lifting me off my feet. I hit him everywhere I could to no avail. He backed us in as the door started closing.

I was still hitting him with desperate fury as he turned an threw me down the hall. I came down sideways on a carpet that slowed me a bit, but not enough to stop it and my head from sliding forehead first in a wall.

I can't say which one I saw first; the darkness or the red stars.

Chapter 6

I awakened in a plain-black wooden chair facing a man, medium build, sitting behind a grey metal desk. He had a black beard. *Black Beard, I thought, was a pirate who*... I came to and tried to get up, but was shoved back down by the shoulders by two powerful hands behind me. I turned my head and gave by best glare at the same muscleman who threw me away.

"Touch me again and I'll kill you", I said to him.

The man behind the desk waved to Mr. Muscle to leave the room. I heard a door close behind me.

"Come now, Mr. James. What did you expect to find here? To be greeted with open arms, coffee and cake?"

"No", I said. "I expected a nunnery, Mister. Nothing more. You guys can learn to be a little nicer. I mean, throwing a guy against the wall ain't exactly friendly. I just had a few questions for the Mother". I felt my forehead. It began to throb.

"And what questions do you come to ask, most gracious detective?", he said.

"So, you know my name and my business too, I bet. That's interesting, but you still had your man ruff me up?"

"Careful, Mr. James", he replied. "Marvin is not as dumb as he looks. Your remark about him not being a monk must have angered him. He's, our security. One look at him and most people get scared and just turn around and go. Not you, it seems".

"Oh, I'm afraid of him alright. That's what I don't like", I said as I squirmed in my chair trying to get comfortable and failing.

"Enough of this sweet talk", I said. "Who told you about me and where's the girl, Mr. Fatman."

"Ouch. I'm not fat, Mr. James. What girl?", he said.

"Come on. You knew I was coming and you know my name. It follows that you must know why I'm here."

He stood up and leaned over his desk to me. "First off, my name is Emerson Carson. That's *Mister* Carson to you, smart guy. Sure, I know why you're here. The fact that you are here presents a problem".

He sat down. "And the fact that you're still alive says a lot too, and don't you forget it!"

"Alive! You bet your butt I'm still alive! And I mean to *stay* alive! Who told you I was coming!?"

"How we know is not important", Mr. Carson said

I reached into my coat and for grabbed my .32, surprisingly it was still there. I had it out and pointed at the man's chest as I stood up.

"Ok, screw it, just bring me the girl and we'll just tippy-toe out of here like real quiet and nobody will get hurt!"

Mr. Carson started to laugh. First a low chuckle that spread through his body till he was shaking all over. Hell, it was a very friendly laugh and I'm a sucker for a good laugh. I starting laughing too.

Still laughing, I walked to him, put the safety on, and threw the gun on his desk. I backed up and sit down still laughing. Running my hand through what hair I had, I let it pause over my face and kind of peeked through my fingers at an unexpected sight. Mr. Carson was pointing the .32 at me. I couldn't figure how he got it and looked around the chair for it, then back at the *Mister* Carson.

He was not smiling now as I saw he was going to pull the trigger. He did, but there was only a click. He started laughing again. I saw nothing funny.

"You son of a bitch", I said. "I could have blown your head off!".

"With an unloaded gun? We unloaded it while you, eh, slept. I wanted to see just how far you would go for your *client*".

"Ok, so now you know. Can we go now?", I said frustrated.

"I'm afraid that is not so simple, Mr. James."

He reached in his desk, took out a loaded magazine. He shoved it, rather roughly I thought, into my .32. I didn't like that.

He stood up and gave it to me. I slipped it my coat holster feeling a little silly.

I offered him my hand and said, "My name is......James, Private Detective".

He offered his back and as we shook hands he said "Emerson Samuel Carson, the 2nd, US Central Intelligence Agency".

I stopped in mid-shake and rolled my eyes to the ceiling and sat down. "Oh, no. What have I got in now?"

"Well, as a friend of mind once said "deep *Kimchi*", I cannot let Marie go because she works for us now. She's really, eh, Top Secret. Actually, beyond that. All I can do is assure you that she's fine, well cared for, and even happy".

"Are you expecting me to go back and tell a worried Mother that? You must know who Mommy is, Mr. Carson. I got two weeks, no twelve days, to bring her back or it's my butt", I replied.

"I can understand Big Sam's motherly instincts, but you must understand that Marie has no Mother and needs no Mother".

"That's the second time I've heard that nonsense about her not having parents! Let me tell you something", I said leaning forward and putting both my hands on his desk.

"Big Sam, that gangster female masquerading as a man is, as far as I'm concerned, Marie's mother!

She acts like a Mother, talks like a Mother, and to make things worse she's got the goons with the guns to back up what she wants".

"Calm yourself. What you say is true but Marie can*not* have a Mother. Not in the tradition sense that is. Marie is a *clone,* Mr. James".

Good thing I was sitting down.

That's it, I thought. Now I had heard it all and if I would not be sitting down, I'd have been on the floor and might have hurt myself. As it was, my eyes fluttered, I slumped forward and began to lose conscience. Mr. Carson rushed to catch me. I guess he did because my head didn't hit the desk.

Chapter 7

I came to looking at the floor and asked breathlessly, "How long was I out"?

"Just a few minutes", answered a female voice. I was face-to-face with a young very pretty girl, boy-like and slim. Six-feet tall was my guess.

She wore a one-piece long-armed body outfit of some lusterless, black plastic-fabric. She wore no shoes even though the stone floor must have been cold. She also wore no make-up.

Deep, black, watchful eyes stared back at me, topped by black eye lashes which were further topped by short black straight hair rendered spike-like by a kind of gel. A full breast looked back at me with pointed nipples that seemed to accuse me, or whoever they were pointing to at the moment, of something.

They had a right to point, I thought. But I did not experience what I usually experienced…

"I'm Marie", she said. "What do you want?"

"Hello, Marie", I replied. Your picture doesn't do you justice. Shall we go? Your Mother is waiting."

"How can a picture do "justice?", Marie asked, pondering. "I have no Mother, Mr. James", she said. Her eyes seem to look right through me. "You heard Emerson. It is impossible for me to have a real Mother".

A haze was rising before my eyes. Only I could see it because it was the blossoming green mist of me about to lose my temper. I would have to hurry before I starting shooting everybody in sight.

"Nonsense, most lovely, provocative, and ignorant young girl.

Everyone has a Mother, no matter real or volunteered. Big Sam loves you. A Mother to you she is and wants to be. "Come", I said standing up and reaching for her hand.

"She will not go with you", Emerson said threateningly. "Can't you understand that?"

She said sadly, "I was made, Mr. James. I don't know exactly how. They won't even tell me how I was made. I was educated here, day and night. What a grind. I had enough when I was sixteen and escaped. I was on the streets for three years before Big Sam found me".

She was crying, her perfect face expressionless and full of tears. "She was nice to me, real nice.

You're right when you say she loves me. But I'm not her *real* daughter, Margo is. Margo was jealous of me the whole time and I guess I made things harder on her because of her life of crime. A life I'm sure she doesn't like. Hell, I'm soft myself and Big Sam, I mean, Marlena, tried to mold me in to something she could not make out of Margo.

"Marlena finally gave up and bought me dolls and doll houses to play with. They were ok, for a while but damn, I was twenty when she found me and the time for dolls was…over? Besides, I wanted to be hard, like Margo.", she said.

"Three years on the streets", I said reflectively. "How long did you live with Big Sam?"

"Almost five years", Marie said.

"And you've been in this so-called nunnery here how long this time?"

"A little over two years", she said with an undercurrent of contempt.

"So, that makes you at least twenty-six years old. You're legally past adult age Marie! In this state that means you're over 21, an adult, and can do what you damn well please!", I said

"What do you mean by that "*adult*" crap?", interrupted Emerson.

"You know exactly what I mean. *Mister* Emerson", I said. "You can't legally hold her here if she's of age and if it's against her will". The last I said directly to Marie. Those pretty black eyes widened a little then relented.

"I'm a creature, Mr. James. A monster. A made thing", Marie said.

"Well, even a *made* thing has rights", I told her. "Come along with me and I'll fix it so you'll never think of yourself as a *made thing* again".

She brightened at that but Mr. Carson said, "Don't be ridiculous, James. She's not going anywhere and if you don't stop talking crazy, neither are you!"

"You idiot! How you people let her escape in the first place? Can't you see that being in the real world only confused her more? Better she was never born, or made or whatever! And who gave you the right to make her anyway!

"*I didn't make her*", Emerson replied emphasizing each word. "The government has the right, and the might, to make experiments of its own choosing. Besides, you don't know all the facts. Look at her, man. She looks like an ordinary female, doesn't she? She's not! She has the strength of twenty, thirty, men. Even we don't know her full potential. She learns faster, runs faster, and heals faster than any woman or human for that matter. She's special. Sure, she's confused and a little confused", he said pointing to his head, "up here. But she's ours!"

"That's why", he said, she must stay here and relearn things. Then we'll find some...*work* for her talents".

"Ah", I mocked him. "You're talking *military* uses, aren't you, Mr. Emerson! I bet you all made her for that purpose, to kill. Am I right? But you've failed her. I can take her to a Mother who'll love and care for her, a friend who can make her forget that she's..."

"And a lover who can take care of her *other* needs, hey Mr. James?", Mr. Carson interrupted. "I saw how you look at her. You think you can help here by bedding her?"

Chapter 8

I lowered by head, somewhat ashamed. "Well…guilty as charged, but just to a point. When I say "friend" I didn't mean *me*! Is that all you got, Mr. Carson? Marie is a still human being.

Whatever I feel for her has to wait until…, yes, that's it! I want you to think about something, Mr. Carson. *Why* are we here on this earth?"

He looked at me blankly.

"To *help* each other!", I said. "Sure, the small things in life you have to figure out how to help yourself, but this, this, is *big*. This…person you *made* is on a higher plane, her problem is bigger than you and me because she needs more help than a normal person!"

"What the *Hell* are you talking about?", Mister Emerson said, "I don't give a damn about no "higher planes". She is a thing to be managed and she will stay here!"

"She needs help. *Our* help, and we are in a position to give her that help. Don't you see! If we don't do anything for her, *we* revert to animals and *she* could become something out of control. If we don't try to guide her through our human…mess, we're less than what she is and... *What are you doing!*", I screamed.

While I was talking and prancing, he had moved to grab her and stuck a gun in her side.

"Now you listen!", Emerson said. "I don't have time for philosophy or religious views! This person is United States government property. She cost a lot of money and I am charged with the protecting and managing the interests of the government. You of all people should know that! After all you yourself used to work for us!"

"*Never* like this, Brother. One of the reasons I quit was because you guys seem to forget that you work for everybody. Everyone would be against this cloning business!" The green-haze was getting thicker as I reached slowly for my gun.

"*Stop!*", he said. "Go for that and I swear I'll shoot you!" He moved her over to his desk where he reached under it and pressed a button.

A deep voice came out of nowhere and said, "Yes, Carson, I've heard it all".

"What are your instructions, Sir?", Carson asked.

"Well, as unfortunate as it seems, they both need to be, er, disposed of!"

"Yes, sir. I thought so too".
"Do it quickly", the voice replied. "Execute the code when it's done. Too bad that you have to eliminate one of your own."

There was a click and then silence.

"One of your own", Marie said barely audible.

"*One of your own!*", she screamed. "You bastard! You're a clone too?

"So, what?", Emerson said. "You've gone bad, so bad that you may not be any use to us.

That's unfortunate, but after all you're still only a woman and...".

She made a massive swing at him. He ducked. The swing would have taken his head off.

Face to face, she asked him, "Why didn't you tell me? We

could have helped each other!"

"I don't need *your* help", he said vehemently. "I am fully integrated into society. I am perfect and one day the world will be totally populated by us. Us! We are the stronger, we are the smarter! *"You could have been with of us!"*

He reached up quickly to throttle her throat.

"You are tainted and imperfect anyway", Mr. Emerson said. "You've seen too much of the outside world at too early an age. If you had waited just two more years, you would have never even thought of escape. You would have seen our superiority. I would've saw to that. Now, you're just soon to be materiel that will be recycled!".

I watched helplessly has he started to choke her in earnest but she broke the hold by smashing her knee in his groin. He doubled and as he straightened, she swung to hit him in the face.

Emerson avoided the blow effortlessly, mockingly. Then he touched her right-side, a small thing to my eyes, but it sent Marie flying across the room strike the wall. I stood dumbly and remembered my gun. He remembered me then and was bringing up his gun to shot me as my first slug hit him.

I walked toward him, emptying the clip in his body. His gun fell to the floor and he stared at me in surprise. He then looked at the holes in his chest and marveled at the bright red fluid flowing from his chest. He fell backwards.

Like a fool I ran to him, forgetting how strong he was, but one look told me he was not long for this world. "Looks like your superiority is not helping you. You're dying", I said.

"Dying? No, impossible, this can't be! I thought...Yes, I am dying", he replied incredulously. "So, this is what it means to die. I feel cold, yet…warm. Is this…normal?"

"I guess so.", I said. "I'm really sorry".

"*You??....* sorry? Why are you sorry?", he said.

"That's…just how I am".

It's ok", he said. Looking up at me he said, "What happens now? Soul? Yes, a soul! Clones must have a soul…just like normal human beings, don't you think?"

He coughed and more blood was on his white shirt.

"Well,", I said, "the people who made you did the best they could, but a soul? That would have had to come from somewhere else, and…well, yeah, of course. Clone or no, I say you have a soul".

"Really", he gasped, eyes glazing over white and fast. "Do you think so? That's wonderful…. you think I'll go to Heaven or to…"

"To Heaven for sure", I said.
"Why? How…how do you know that?", he asked.

"Not your fault", I said.

"Good ar---gu---ment, I'm...*what's that coming*?", he said, raising his white-eyes to the ceiling.

I looked up quickly but all I saw was ceiling. By the time I turned back to him he was dead. Whatever he saw up there was for him alone.

Just then Marvin came in, took everything in at a glance and came for me. His intent was to kill me but Marie stepped in between us. Marvin hesitated for a moment and then bored in toward us.

He reached for her, missed. She ducked under his outstretched arms. I watched in awe as the hundred-pound Marie picked up

49

the three-hundred-pound Marvin and slammed him to the floor.

It was fortunate for him that she did not throw him head first; it would have killed him. As it was, she stood over the unconscious man and I had to hurry to stop her as she lifted her foot deliberately over his head.

"No!", I managed to burp out and hurried to her. "No time for more fun. Let's get out of here." I took her hand and we ran to an opened door, and down the hall. Curiously, there was no pursuit, no blaring alarms. "How many others in this *convent?*" I asked her as we ran.

"Just the three of us", Marie said.

I stopped. "Are you kidding? Just you three in this big building? Where are the rest?"

"Off.", was her reply. That explains it I thought and its typical. Big government building–few employees.

We got to the front-vault door. There were no knobs that I could see but Marie walked right up to it. She bent and reached under the door, moving fingers left and right.

A low hiss of air and the door opened toward us. I could see my car parked tantalizingly in front of us.

It looked inviting close as we shot through the front door as if chased by demons.

I had a hard time keeping up with Marie.

I got to the car and reached in my pockets for the keys, but no keys. Incredibly they were dangling innocently in the ignition. I had never done that before. I looked over at the house and we were still not pursued. We jumped in the car, I started the engine, turned around and drove recklessly down the road.

Chapter 9

We drove toward the city without incident, but I was expecting a chase. Any second I thought we'd be stopped by battalions of cops, G-men, and assorted other government heavies.

But then I realized they could pick us up anytime they wanted to. Where could we hide? They must know that I would be easy to find, because I was not the hiding type. As for Marie, well I got the impression that she was just too naive to hide and I couldn't force her too anyway.

What she did to Marvin…Mr. Muscle..."Heck", I said aloud, startling Marie, and slowed the car down. We were getting close to Hoochie's place anyway. I must have been thinking of him the whole drive.

Hoochie, a good friend, was a midget and an ex-master hypnotist. He had made a lot of money and was in a kind self-imposed retirement. He had quit because he was too good and had begun to hate his audience and the show. It seemed that Hoochie was not only a hypnotist but a dabbler in the occult; not quite a warlock but the mixture of hypnotism and witchcraft almost drove him crazy.

His career came to screeching halt some years ago when he left a sixty-year-old female aristocrat in a dire way, and simply walked off the stage. The fact that she had asked to be hypnotized, saying aloud from the audience that she "did not believe in this silly hocus-poscus" was no excuse for what Hoochie did to her. In full view of the audience, he not only hypnotized her but got her down on all fours running all over the stage screaming "I'm a chicken! eat me, eat me, fuck me!" at the top of her lungs, interspersed with dog barks.

The next day they found Hoochie, who was not hiding, and for a promise of immunity from prosecution, and being sued for all he had, he brought the woman back to normal; whatever that was for her. When she was told what she had been doing for the last 24 hours, she fainted.

Hoochie had simply stepped over her and walked away.

I was glad that he had decided to live in the deep forest because I didn't want to show my face in town, not just yet.

I was one of few who knew where he lived and he made me swear that I'd tell no one. I turned off the main road to a dirt road that you had to know it was there or you'd drive right by it. I drove for another 10 miles in deep woods and there it was, "Hoochie House".

That's what he liked to call it. It was made of barked wood that helped to camouflage it.

I stopped the car and studied the house. On the front porch two large black wolves stood on eight-legs and studied me back. One wolf turned its head to the other as if to ask "*Lunch?*".

The other wolf turned its head back to it as if to say "*No. Visitor*".

We got out of the car, the motor sighed its happiness to rest, as I walked around it to stand next to Marie. By then Hoochie, former entertainer and still a midget, was standing on the porch watching us.

I had not noticed him there and couldn't figure out if he had been there all the time or had he just come through the walls.

We walked together toward the house. "Let me do the talking", I said to her out of the corner of my mouth. She didn't reply and I noticed then that she was smiling. First time I'd seen that.

"Hoochie!", I called.

"James, you bastard", came the distinguished but disinterested reply. Nobody noticed me anymore. All eyes were on Marie.

The wolves studied her with whimsical looks, inclined their heads first to the left and then to the right, as if studying some new phenomena. They both sat down with the effort.

Hoochie had a curious look on his face. "Where the *Hell* did you get her?" he said as one of the wolves whined as if asking the same question.

"Quiet", he said and both wolves stretched out.

"Found her. Her name is Marie", I replied.

Hoochie started down the steps to us. The wolves, starting up, were about to follow him but he stopped them with a backward raise of the hand. He walked straight up to her, looking up to her face. Marie didn't move and stared down at him. They stared at each other intently. Both wolves whined now, but this time Hoochie didn't stop them.

"She ain't real, James".

"She's real enough", I said.

"Come down to me my child", he said. Marie went to her knees and they stared at each other more, almost nose to nose for a long time.

I was about the interrupt when he said "All right, stand up".

Marie stood up.

"I need your help Hoochie", I said to him as they stared at each other. "Something that I'll pay you for. Something that would do her a great deal of good". As I began to explain everything, he walked around her as she looked to the wolves. I finished explaining and he came to me, his eyes eying the ground, his hands behind his back.

"*Great deal of good*", he repeated flatly to me. "I dreamed last night that someone would say that to me". He looked me up and down as if seeing me for the first time. "James! How's it hanging! Ain't seen you in... what? Ten years?!"

"Yeah", I said, "Being out in this air is making me nervous."

He looked at me sharply. "Cops?"

"Worse".

"Worse? Ain't nothing worse than cops".

"*Government* cops", I said.

"Damn", he grinned. "You're right. Come on in". We started for the house and I remembered the wolves.

"What about the Brothers Grimm", I pointed.

Both wolves stood and turned their muzzles to look at me.

"They ain't brothers, there're a pair and won't harm no one unless I tell em." He looked at Marie. "They'll do what you tell them to do also, I think".

"Schulta Hukiwiii!", he said to them and both left the porch in bounds and went to Marie. She reached down and stroked them both. They laid on their backs and she stroked their stomachs. Finally, one after the other, they both stood on their hind legs, paws on Marie's shoulders and licked her face. The whole time I just noted their teeth. They seemed to have a lot.

"I guess they like each other!", Hoochie said pointing to them. He glanced back at me and saw that my hand was in my coat for gun that shoots.

"Take your hand out real slow, Mister James, and never do that again!", Hoochie hissed. "They'd tear you to pieces if they saw that play!"

I complied.

"Alright, alright", he said to the wolves with both hands out. "That's enough fun". One got down from Marie's shoulder and both looked to him. He said to them, "Rabbit! Lady and Gentleman! I don't care how many you eat but I need three, ok? Now go get em!", Hoochie ordered.

The wolves came to him, rubbing their furry bodies around his legs, him reaching down to pet and stroke them. Hoochie bent down and they nosed each other and in a flash the wolves took off through the woods.

"They don't seem to be in a hurry", I said jokingly. "I'll pass on the rabbit."

"They never are and you, my dear friend, can eat lousy hot dogs".

Chapter 10

The wolves brought us three rabbits. Hoochie did the cooking, and as he and Marie ate, I went over my plan again. He didn't bat an eye and when I told her she was a clone he just said "Ahhhh!", as if that explained everything. "I bet they made her first", he observed.

"Well, I don't really know. But you probably right, us men always think we are first in everything", I replied.

Hoochie shook his head.

"Anyway, I decided to come to you. I know you were once a great hypnotist...", I said.

"Still am, sir".
"Ok", I replied.

"What's a hypnotist?", Marie asked.

"Never mine dear", said Hoochie. "By the way aren't you getting sleepy?"

Hoochie and she locked eyes again and the silent battle of wills went on. Marie was strong. But I thought she had no chance against Hoochie. She resisted for some moments but her eyes closed. She was about to fall in her plate as I gently grabbed her.

"Wake-up and eat, Marie", Hoochie ordered. She woke up and finished the meal as if nothing had happened.

"It will be difficult", he said

"I know, but I want you to do is give her a new life, Hoochie, somewhere far from her. Fix it so she won't remember what she is".

"I see. And what you say to all that, my dear?", Hoochie asked Marie.

They locked again and I was glad I was not between them.

She said, "I say that you and I are alike. We're both freaks but understand each other.

Teach me what I need to know so I won't just starting killing people for the fun of it...that thought is deep within me. It's trying to get it out".

"I get that feeling also to start killing people. Selectively of course", I said.

Hoochie glared at me to shut-up.

"Marie", he replied, "there's a chance that I might fail you, my dear. You are very perceptive person and intelligent, but I am not perfect. The fact that you're willing to listen to me might make the difference. You're right about us being freaks. But there are degrees to freakdom; there are good freaks and there are bad freaks, the difference in your case being that you don't have a purpose in life, and that puts you in the middle, meaning, of course that you can go good, or go bad.

"We all need purpose in life, Marie, or else all we have is confusion and a lot of other ugly things. I think your makers were so obsessed with secrecy that they forgot to tell you yours. Call that an error for the sake of argument and you see what happens when Man plays God and Man ain't no damn good at it!! However, I'd say that me and you are good freaks and are certainly better off than the general populace!", Hoochie said laughingly.

"Spare me please, O super beings!", I interrupted. They turned to me. "Let's not get that *superior than thou* attitude, ok? You both can stay freaky. Just tone it down".

Marie laughed and said, "Ok".

"Aren't you tried, Marie?", Hoochie said and pointed to a room behind her. "Go to that room. There's a bed there. Lock the door and lie down", he told her.

Marie stood and stretched her 6-foot fine frame, her finger tips almost touching the ceiling, her back arching, her firm breasts pointing... I looked away. Out of the corner of my eye I could see Hoochie smile and slowly shake his head.

Marie turned and went to the bedroom.

"How did you get her to go to bed like that?", I asked.

"Wouldn't you like to know! *That* was no special power, Milton. She's obviously tired. I just showed her where the bed was", he grinned. "For minute there I thought you were going to put your fingers up in the sign of the cross as she was stretching, warding off a vampire or something", he grinned.

"Go to Hell. I am clear on her. I can't have her, nor do I really want her", I grinned back.

"How much?", I asked him.

"How much what? You mean *money*? Don't insult me, James. I'll do this for nothing. Won't cost you a cent".

"How noble", I said.

"Look at who's calling *me* noble! I'll never be as nice as you", he said. "You bring a helpless, beautiful, young, sexy, and innocent girl, a rarity in itself, here whom you like and you just *give her to me*! But you did the right thing, James she's special and I don't think our government knew what it had in its hands. She's a pistol, Milton, a weapon that can be trained to do anything. Very dangerous in the wrong hands!", he said and stopped talking to stir what was in left on his plate, thinking.

"You saw how she charmed my wolves, or they charmed her! No one has ever done that before. Yep, very special indeed. Just the privilege of formulating what to teach her…why that's payment enough!" he said laughing.

"Ok, ok, but how you going to do it?", I asked.

"Don't have a damn clue my friend, but If I can't do it in a week..." He shrugged. "She'll be the daughter I never had. She'll be asking some strange questions, but no matter. She'll have a base to live on; the freedom of normalcy, whatever that is with me. I'll have to teach her to hide her physical strength though".

I gave him a funny look and he replied "Yes, yes, my friend. I saw her physical strength before you told me of it. After her training, I'll send her to my relatives in Europe. Thank you, Mr. James".

"Thank you, Mr. West", I replied. We both laughed.

"It's getting late, Hoochie, and as much as I'd like to stay and talk with you, I need to get to town" I said. "Say…will she remember me?"

"Do you want her too, Mister James?", Hoochie replied.

"No. It's better she forgets me".

"Well, that may or may not be better, I'll try to do that but it might not work. I can see that she's kind of fond of you".

I sat there biting my lower lip.

"Milton, she'll know Big Sam, me, plus a few others. There're things that can't be erased or forgotten", Hoochie said. He stood up and I could hear scratching at the front door.

"She'll be fine! Now get out of here and come see me when the smoke's cleared."

I stood up also and reached to shake the hand he offered. I turned to go out the front door, but to my surprise Marie stood there in front of it, arms folded, a disapproving look first to me and then to Hoochie. *Good Lord*, I thought. She had opened her bedroom door and come back in the room without us hearing or seeing her. I turned to admonish Hoochie, but I could see that was upset and concerned.

He too had not heard her and realized that she would be a very tough nut to crack.

"I'll never forget you, nor do I want to forget you", she said calmly.

I swallowed. "You'll have to sweetheart. I'm no good for you. In my line of work, I don't even have time for you. Best you..."

"And if I won't?", she asked. "Remember, I do what I want", she said.

"Hoochie will make sure you do", I replied.

She glanced at Hoochie and smiled and he smiled back. "Even he cannot do everything. You forget that I am a superior being!"

She started laughing at that and we couldn't help joining in. We laughed all the way out the front door to the porch, but as I started down the steps the laugher died a natural death. It was dark out. Maybe that's what stopped it.

I went deliberately to the car, knowing full well that if I hesitated, I'd go back to the house and straight to Marie's arms; like the love-sick puppy that I was.

I made it to the car, got in, turned the ignition, and drove away.

As I looked back, in the rear-view mirror, I could see them both standing there. Only Hoochie waved.

Then I realized that I was so intent on getting away that I had totally forgot about the Brothers Grimm. But they had been the scratching on the door as if to say; "Time to go. No place for you her, strange human". Yes, they were with me escorting my sorry self-down the road, one on each side of the car.

Jealous bastards, I thought.

Chapter 11

As I drove down the dirt road, my emotions were turning, bending, swirling, and blending with their typical confusion. I was either in love or my stomach was playing games due to the hot-dogs.

In love indeed, I thought, as I played with the real answer knowing its impossibility. *However, could I be in love with Margo?* No.

She had struck a chord but I knew it was pity I felt for her. Pity that she was in something she could not get out of and simple, unreliable, lust. Big Sam? No way.

She was attractive in a brutal sort of way, but attraction it was nevertheless, the kind where you knew you were playing with fire but could not resist the flame that would eventually kill the moth.

Marie? Yes, but best to ignore the stir as I was attempting to do. Hootchie saw it and I knew it all the time. Just the mention of her name bought depression, deep melancholy. Then I thought, *this is what we men get when we start to compare women...comparing was a waste of time...*

"Damn!", I said aloud. "I got that sickness again".

But this time I would not let the four-letter word rot my insides away by longing for someone I couldn't have. This time I had a protector; a shield called *distance,* oh, sweet distance, how putrid is thy sting, thou fake *Corrector* of all maladies.

All this went through my head as I drove up to Big Sam's place. In deep thought I did not notice that the Moon was obscured by...smoke? Yes!

Where the house stood there was a smoking ruin. The roof had fallen in. Black tendrils rose everywhere, some beckoning to me, dark and heavy oily smoke snaking up to the sky, casually fleeing through the front-door's vault that now lay on the ground like some dead black monster. The smoke-snake arched languidly back and forth up to the Moon and played peek-a-boo with it. But the Moon didn't care about no damn smoke, *it* had all the time in the universe.

I drove on and noticed Harvey walking back from the house to his lone unmarked police car. I honked and pulled up next to him and get out.

"Harvey! What happened?", I asked breathlessly.

He studied me for a span and said, "Well, well, if it ain't Mr. Smart Guy. Ain't it funny, you showing right this minute. Like you maybe had something to do with this?".

"Oh, no, don't try to pin this me! I didn't have anything to do with this!", I said. "Know who did?"

Harvey relaxed. "Not exactly" he said and we both turned to look at the house. I could see that there had been a huge explosion. The right-side of the house was a pile of stone and the remaining blacked walls on the left side conspired to hold each other up and what was left of roof. I wouldn't go in there for all the tea in China. The sky cleared and the Moon shone full on the ruin. Water used to put out the fire glistening like sprayed plastic. There was sizzling that sounded like anguished breathing, as if structure was moaning for mercy.

The explosion must have obliterated everyone in the house. They didn't have a chance. Curious though, that the smell of burned flesh was absent.

"Find anyone in that?", I said pointing to the wrecked building.

"Yeah. A man and a woman. Leg here, head there. The rest charred. Terrible", Harvey replied.

"Woman dressed in black?"

"Yeah, I guess so, the dress melted in the flesh…".

"Big Sam and Earl", I said.

Harvey turned to me.

"Get real, James. You still think Big Sam was a dame? No way, pal. Big Sam's a guy and as far as *we're* concerned the guy, we pulled out of there *is* Big Sam, and good riddance! The woman, well, just an innocent bystander".

"You really don't know who did this?", I asked again.

"Hell, should I know? The Captain thinks it was the competition. Lord knows the bad guys been shooting each other up a lot over territory".

"Your Captain...", I began.

"Ain't very bright, I know. But this time he got it right. The house is proof. We found a lot of shell casings, different calibers. In the house and outside. There was a big shootout before the explosion. Dynamite or whatever it was. Hell man, we could hear it clear to town".

I exhaled a long breath. "Harvey, I got something to tell ya and it stays between you and me, ok?" I gave him the full poop, starting from the visit to my office by Big Sam's boys. I didn't tell him where Marie was.

He didn't say anything for a long time. "Ok", he said. "Let's say I buy your crazy story. Where's the girl?"

"On the Moon", I said.

"Oh" he said putting both hand on his hips. "The first girl on the moon, heh? Come on, give it to me and come clean or you'll be the first *man* on the Moon or it's to jail you go!".

"You can take me anywhere you want, Copper!", I knew that would get to him. "It's for your own good, Harvey. The less you know the better".

He made a move toward me, but I said "Hold on, we got company!". Down the road came two large black cars, the same kind that I had taken a ride in with Margo and Earl. Harvey and I reached inside our coats.

The cars came to a screeching halt in front of us. The doors opened and slammed shut in staccato time. When they were all out, I counted twenty-five, black-suited guys.

They surrounded us in their version of it, which was half-circle, and every Mother's Son of them carried a Tompkins machine gun, all pointing at us.

What a sight; a smoldering house behind us, a bunch of soon to be smoking guns in the front. We eased our gun-hands back in view. Two guys came briskly forward.

They stopped in front of us. Harvey said loudly while pointing at the group, "I hope them guys got *permits* for those things". It was all I could do to keep from laughing.

"Who are you people and what happened here?", one black-suited guy asked.

"Police Detective Lieutenant Harvey Miller, you hear me! Organized Crime Division", Harvey blustered and pointed to me, "This here is Private Detective James, who really has no damn business here just like you guys! And who might you guys be?".

Whoever these two are they're dumb, I thought. They're right in front of us. If any shooting started, they'd be the first to get it…

"And what happened here?", asked the other testily.

"We got an echo here or what! Police business!", replied Harvey. "If you want to know more you need to come downtown. While we're being cozy like, I'll ask you again; who the hell are you guys! Let me see some identification!"

"That'll have to wait, Lieutenant. Here comes more", I said.

Indeed. Down the road came four more cars of the same type and color. They screeched to a halt behind the other cars but only ten guys got out. They were not armed and mingled and mixed with the others. Some evidently knew each other.

One of the newly arrived strolled up, looked to each of us and said, "Agent Kenneth Doe, Central Intelligence Agency".

That topped the cake and even Harvey was too surprised to say anything. Harvey introduced us again. The two other agents introduced themselves.

"Agent John Smith, Federal Bureau of Investigation".

"Agent John Doe, Federal of Investigation".

Harvey groaned.

I could not resist pointing to the two Doe's. "You two brothers or something?", I asked.

"No, we're not!", replied the Agent Doe of the FBI Doe.

I looked sharply at him. I'd heard that voice before and now, in the gathering light of dawn, I finally put one and zero together and finally recognized Earl.

"Well, well. Mr. Earl, the tough guy. So, you're FBI undercover, huh? That explains a lot. How long you work for Big Sam?", I asked.

Mr. Smith answered, "Five years and he didn't like it a bit, I assure you".

"You assure me", I said with all the smirk I could muster. "Now that's very nice, Mr. Earl. How many people did you ice for Big Sam and Miss Justice?"

"None of your damn business, you two-bit small-timer. I'll tell you this; I came close to icing *you*!", Earl said.

"Shut up, *Agent* Doe!", Mr. Smith said sharply. He walked to me and using his finger for emphasis he poked my chest saying, "*Where-is-Marie*, Mr. James!"

"Yes, where is Marie, Mr. James", repeated the CIA man Kenneth Doe. "By the way, gentlemen", he said smoothly, "I am taking over this investigation. Any objections?"

Mr. Smith said, "I object. However, I know that since you are here, and I don't like it that you are here, there's nothing I can do but say…. go right ahead and take over…it's your career, not mine, *Kenny*!"

Silence.

Mr. Kenneth Doe of the CIA did not bat an eye. "It's nothing to *do* with career, *JohnBOY!* I have superior federal authority here. You may file your *objection* whenever and with whomever you chose. You understand me?"

Before understanding had a chance, Harvey spoke up, "Well now, this *MaaRie* or whatever the Hell her name is, is wanted for questioning and is a fugitive from the law, *our l*aw! I got two dead bodies in that house over there and who knows how many more gonna just pop-up! I demand to talk to her like proto. Get it!".

"Matter of fact", Harvey went on by sweeping his hand over the whole group, "Maybe I'll arrest you *all* you guys and we'll take a little jaunt to headquarters! You're out of your jurisdiction!"

A deadly silence. The Tommies were still pointed at us. No

cricket made a sound. At last, several of the men snickered.

"Quiet!", said Agent Smith turning to scream.

The Kenneth, the CIA man said, "The whole United States is *our* jurisdiction, Mr. James. I am sure that Agent Doe agrees with me that this Marie is very dangerous and she belongs to the people who…developed her. You hear *me* Mr. James, *Detective Lieutenant Miller*? Both of you are mixing in government, I repeat gentlemen, serious government business. I suggest you cooperate before I have to take *you* somewhere for questioning!"

"First off", I said, "I can suggest where *you* can go for questioning!

Second, all you ass-holes is crowding me, so back off or I'll drill ya where you stand. Could be a whole lot of nasty shooting you'd have to explain", I said reaching in my coat. Harvey did the same.

The three agents backed up a step.

"I'm a guy with just some of the answers", I continued talking. "You deal with me!"

Neither of the three said anything.

"Understand!", I said louder got their mumbled assent. "Now, Agent Earl or whatever your damn name is, I want you to verify to the good Police Detective here that Big Sam *is* a woman."

Earl hesitated, but Agent Doe nudged him.

"Yeah, damn you", Earl replied. "Big Sam *is* a woman. So, what does that have to do with anything? We are not after her! We all want Marie! She escaped from a government facility, she is government property, that's all there is too it. The powers that be sent all of us to find her and we will have her! You two guys don't know what you messing with. She's *unpredictable*! She's *dangerous*! A ticking time-bomb, she must be further…studied…oh *Hell and Damn it ALL!*" He turned to the small army. "Lower your weapons and put them on safe"!"

Twenty-five guys FBI men lowered their Tommies. I noticed the CIA guys took their hands out of their upper coat pockets.

"Good", I said. "That's all I wanted".

"And the girl", asked Mr. Smith.

"What girl?", I replied.

Exasperated, Mr. Smith replied, "This matter is way over your head, Mr. James. Now, be nice and tell us where she is and we'll forget your part in it. I mean, after all, I add one person to the body count, that makes *three* dead bodies with another person somewhat mentally damaged. You could be put jailed for a very, very, long time, *Mister* James".

He looked to Harvey for agreement but Harvey was silent.

"Mr. Smith, of the government for the people and by the people", I said. "I have no idea what you are talking about. I was hired by Big Sam, at the point of gun, to find her daughter. Turned out that she didn't *have* a daughter. The death of my client means the case is closed. I can't by law and client privilege give you any information without my client's permission."

Harvey snickered. I glared at him to shut up.

I could see that Earl was getting hot about the whole thing.

"Don't play games you damn fool!", Mr. Smith said. "Big Sam was a small-time crook of no consequence to us. She's dead now and you don't have to protect her anymore", he said.

"On the contrary, Mister. For me and this city she was big time. But let you people tell it we're all small time. Big Sam gets the same confidentially and service all my clients get under the law".

"Law!", shouted Earl. "Whose damn law?"

"*My* law!", I replied. It went silent again and this time I thought this was it. I drew myself up and yawned. "Gentlemen", I said, "I'm getting in my car and leaving. You guys are starting to bore me". I made not a single step because like magic all the guns came up.

Even John, Mike, and John had hands in their coats.

There we all stood; three guys in black suits, me in my old tweed coat and jeans, Harvey in rumpled grey, surrounded by twenty-five guys in black suits all armed with Tommie guns. The newly arrived, in various states of dress, were pointing .38 pistols at us.

Behind them all were their silly cars, patiently waiting like black obedient beetles. Beyond them was freedom, a long way off just now.

"Hey!", I said, both palms out. "You can't start shooting here! He's a cop and I'm a private citizen. How you gonna EX-plain that to the public? You can't *accident* things away all the time."

I watched Harvey as he reached slowing in his vest and said, so all could hear, "I swear you three will be the first to go down!".

"Me too" I said after making the ultimate craziness of reaching in for my .38 pistol.

It started to rain. Maybe that decided it, maybe not. John, the CIA man, turned and told the small army again to lower their weapons. "It's over!", he told them. "I want everyone to forget they were here. Now back to the cars! This is the CIA speaking!"

The small army turned to their cars.

"You sure you want to do that", asked John Smith the FBI man in a hostile tone.

"Yes, I do. And what's more I take full responsibility", Agent Kenneth Doe said.

"Ahhh, the magic word, "responsibility", chimed in Earl in a sarcastic tone. "So, it'll be on your head!"

"Yeah", Mr. Smith said dejectedly as he turned to me, "I hope to God you know what you're doing. If word gets out that there's a female clone running loose that cost a few million dollars, with an IQ that's through the roof, *and* has the strength of a bunch of guys...".

"I don't know what you're talking about and I always know what I'm doing. Now please leave", I said.

"Well, I trust the CIA,", Earl said, pointing to me. "I just don't trust *him*! Not for a minute. I got half-a-mind to take him with us. We got ways to make him talk!"

"That's a no, no, brother!", Harvey was saying. "*Him* ain't going nowhere! Mr. James is under arrest. You can have him *after* we're finished with him. Now won't you do like the nice man says and blow and take your damn *half-mind with you*!"

That seemed to can it. Earl and his boss let out exasperated breaths. Turning on their heels to leave, I could hear them both barking orders to their men.

Chapter 12

"One last thing, Copper", Mr. Doe from the CIA said just before getting in a vehicle. "You need to forget that clone exists. Don't tell your Captain or anybody else. Not even your Mother. The secret stays with us, and under the United States Secrets Act, I order you to keep silent about this whole matter under pain of big jail time and a fine! Got that!"

"Got it", Harvey shot back in a clipped tone.

"By the way gents", I said.

They all turned to me. "There's a safe deposit box detailing everything. If something were to happen to me or the Lieutenant here..."

"Nonsense, James. You didn't have time to do that. You're lying", Mr. Doe said waving his arms.

"Am I?", I said.

"And what would be the point of you having it? I told you we'd forget about your involvement".

"Oh, I believe you", I said. "It's just that even you got a boss. He might not agree with you. And let's not discount Earl. He doesn't like me very well. Let's just say the box is insurance".

"I got one too", Harvey said. "Now all of ya get out of here before I give you a ticket or something!"

Mr. Doe started laughing and laughter is catching. His men laughed, too. I wanted very much to laugh myself, but I knew that Harvey would never forgive me.

Mr. Doe, still laughing, waved a good-bye to us from the front-passenger seat. The car turned around and his vehicle was the last to go down the road. Harvey and I stood next to our cars and watched the last dust fade. The rain stopped then as if on que. It was full daylight and I realized we had missed the dawn and had been screwing around all night.

"Well, so much for that! See ya around Harv!", I said as I turned to my car and got in. Harvey followed and stood by the driver's side as I stared the motor.

He slowly stooped down to me and leaning his arm on the sill he said in a vehement voice, "I ought to run your butt in!"

"*Me*!? What in the world for, for Christ's sake!", I replied.

"Leave him out of it, James! I'll think of something. How bout obstruction of justice? Lying to an officer of the law? How bout just plain disturbing the damn peace!! Where-is-the-girl, *Milton*!"

I killed the motor. "Now don't you start, dammit! Don't be stupid Harvey. If I wouldn't tell *them*, what makes you even think I'd tell *you!*

Well, the dumb lug arrested me. I spent the next five days in jail. The charge? "Disturbing the peace", was Harvey's answer. I think he locked me up to protect me because he didn't book me and gave me a key to my cell. The key made it almost like a vacation. Almost.

Chapter 13

On the sixth day Detective Miller let me out of jail officially. I walked the five-miles, I needed the exercise and fresh air, to my office. My office was cold, I had forgotten to leave the heat on. I got the heat going and turned the desk around to face the door, and that's when I noticed the envelope on the floor. I went and got it. It had a foreign address and I sat at my desk to read;

"Your package, Sir, arrived here undamaged but had no return postage. Also, we inform you that all the parts, though undamaged, nevertheless were one short. We may insist, sometime in the distant future, that you supply the missing part that adds some worth to the whole. Otherwise, it works perfect and is manageable. A happy "Go to Hell" from our mutual friend".

Regards,

A. Ramirez-Sanchez

Portugal

I read the letter again. "Damn!", I said aloud. "She really likes me!"

The front door opened without a knock as I said that, a female voice said, "I don't!".

It was Margo. Margo in a tight blue short skirt with white blouse showing a bit of cleavage. Just above her cleavage hung a silver chain with the words "Damn You".

She looked at me with friendly eyes as she closed the door and clopped and drifted to me like a shark, with stiletto high-heals, over my wooden floor. I hoped she was not wearing red high heels. I didn't dare look.

"Thought you were dead", I said getting up.

"Not today!", she said and sat on the edge of my desk. "You like me, don't you?".

"So what? Who killed Big Sam?", I replied sitting down trying to change the subject.

"She ain't dead, you dolt!", Margo said getting up and leaning over the desk, showing me Moons with cleavage that gave me the blues.

"What?", I said surprised.

"Mother is *way* too smart to let us get hemmed in, shot up, or blown up. We both got away, to do crime another day!", she laughed.

"So, what do you do now? What do you want?"

"For now? Just you, Brother. Let's go out and tear this silly town up!", she said.

I backed my chair to the wall. "I don't know if I am up to that kind of fun. How many people have you killed?"

"Not a single one, actually", she said licking her red lips. "It was all an act. I could never kill anyone. I took the job because Mom wanted me to work for my keep. I thought it would be exciting".

"Was it?", I asked.

"Hell no! Most of the time it was boring", she said as she came around my desk, a desk which gave up on me and was no help at all. I stood up and she kicked the chair away and pushed me against the wall.

"I found you, though, quite exciting". She tried to kiss me but I turned away.

"What's the matter? I don't have much time, shake it up, the police must be looking for me. I'll have to get out of town". She was unbuttoning her blouse.

"Believe me they'll never recognize you, not the way I described you. Stop that!", I said as she was about to take off the blouse that obviously did not come with a bra.

She stopped the blouse number. Her disappointment lead to anger. From somewhere she pulled a petit pistol with a red handle. I did not want to be shot with such a gun, I wanted to tell her to go away and come back with a proper cannon.

"The doors behind you", was as all I could manage.

"You don't want me?", she said with a husky voice. "You like Marie, don't you? Dammit! Everybody likes me Marie better than me. Hey…. that kinda rhymes, don't it?"

"Well, yes and no. Could I take a rain-check? Uncle Miltie just ain't in the mood right now", I lied.

Her expression made her instantly ugly, but that reaction was understandable.

"I don't give rain-checks, besides I'm in a hurry. Too bad for you, *Dick*!", still pointing that girly gun at me.

"Yeah, too bad for me", I said as I walked around her and held the door open.

"Did you even find Marie? Mother paid you a lot of money to at least do that".

"Yes, I found her but the FBI took her away from me", I said.

"Really?", she said taking a few steps toward me. "I would think that the CIA would be *more* interested in her. Wouldn't you think so, Mister James?"

"I don't know what you are talking about?", I said with door in hand and looking to the ceiling.

She followed my look to the ceiling, shook her head and looked me in the eye, "Well, again you prove you are not as dumb as you want us to think. You know about Marie. Well, she told Mother what she was just before she ran away and later Mother decided that we really needed dear Marie back as our number one persuader, our muscle because she had a lot. That's one reason she wanted you to get Marie to like come home, or whatever you want to call it. The other reason was she cared and saw Marie as a second Daughter. No skin off my nose, pal. Marie could come and go as she pleased and I'd never miss her. So, where is she?"

"I have no idea. Probably in some deep governmental protection or who knows. The whole caper stinks and is over as far as I'm concerned. I've had enough. Give a big hello to Big Sam next time you see her", I said still holding the door open.

She lowered her gun and said "See you around, dick!", and walked out of my office. She smelled damn good. I closed the door gently and felt that she just stood on the landing, probably hoping I would let her back in. It was unbearable but I waited her out, finally hearing a gentle walk down the stairs.

"Adieu, my dear", I said to the door.

Back at my desk I studied my wooden walls, then the silent door, but before I could really feel sorry for myself a thought floated down from the ceiling.

What the Hell did Sammy Paul, the Pimp, want?

End

"The Jones' is Off My List"

From the Series "Milton C. James, Private Detective (IV)
By Jackie Leverett
Copyright December 1, 2019

I was sitting in my office when a guy comes in, takes a look at me, then pulls a gun.

"Where the hell is he!", the guy said angrily, pointing what looked like some kind of Luger but from where I was sitting it didn't matter what it was. I raised my hands and stood up slowly, friendly like. His gun-hand with that long-barreled pistol came up with me.

"Who?", I managed to croak like squeezing the last drop from a rotten orange.

"The guy that used to sit where you're standing!", he said.

"I been here over ten years", I said.

"You don't know the guy was here when you got here?".

"No", I lied.

He looked at me funny and said, "You're lying".

"How do you know that?", I said

"You're a bad liar, Brother. It's an art and you ain't got it. You got a twitch in your left-eye! Come on, spill!", he said stepping closer pointing the gun at my head.

"The twitch is from the war", I said.

"You were in the war?", he said.

"No, but hearing about it made me nervous like you wouldn't

believe. Every day I thought I'd be invited".

He smiled at that but I still thought he was going to shoot me.

"You a funny guy or just dumb?". He put that girlie gun inside his coat and I could see it was a 9mm Luger. A fancy gun way out of place in this side of town.

He came closer, stopped. "What are you doing? Why don't you put your hands down?".

"I'm scared you might have a knife and throw it at me or something".

"Don't be a chump", he said. "People who have guns don't carry knives".

"Not where I come from", I said.

He chuckled and moved to sit in my customer chair. That didn't make me feel any better. I would have been happy if he'd have just left or had never been born. He looked me up and down, then raised his gun-hand slowly up and down. I got the hint. I put my hands down and sat.

He leaned toward me with a hard look. "You know Renfro Jones"?

An internal alarm went off, reminding me of one of my Grandpa's sayings, "there's a dead-cat on the line" and to watch out. Sure, I knew Renfro Jones but not this guy.

"Never heard of him", I lied again.

He chuckled again. "I think you an honest guy. I might have some work for you."

I'd been called worse but I didn't want anything to with this guy.

"I don't think I could work for you. Actually, I'm up to my butt in work and just don't have time...", I said.

"Yes, you do", he said interrupting me.

"Er, no I'm sure I can't".

He put a hand inside his coat, left it there.

"Oh, I am sure you can, Mister…what's the name?", he asked.

"Do you always reach for a gun when you're trying to make a point?", I asked him.

"Yeah, I do. So, what about it?", he said.

"Never mind", I said. "James is the name. You must have seen it on the signs as you were coming up the stairs, and on my door.", I said pointing to it.

He took his hand out of his coat.

"Didn't see no damn sign and wasn't looking for no damn sign, Mister James".

"Ok, ok. So, what you want done, Mister?"

"Jones, is the name".

"You related to Mr. Renfro?"

"Not on your life, pal, and my name don't matter. Get it?"

"I get it. What's the job?". I hung on to my seat.

"I want you to find this guy you never heard of. He took off with three of my girls, and you tell him I want the money back".

I said nothing. He glared.

"I can understand the money, but what about the three girls?", I asked.

"Don't care about them, he can keep em or adapt em. I don't give a damn.".

"Ok, so just the money back is the message? Is that all?", I asked.

"Nope. That ain't *all*. Tell him if I don't get the money back in two days, I'm gonna send some of my boys to un-arrange his life!"

"By...re-arrange, you mean...?"

"That's UN-arrange, Mister James. He'll know what it means".

"Wonderful", I said. "Can you tell me how much money we talking about here?"

"Forty-thousand big ones, pal", he said with a frown that made him uglier than he was.

I tried to repeat that figure but started coughing.

"That's" …I said still coughing…, "more money than I make in three years".

He looked around my office. "I'm sure of that, pal".

I raised a finger and reached down to open a desk-drawer and took out my bottle of whiskey and put it on the desk. I closed the drawer, still coughing, and reached for the bottle to take a slug.

Mr. Jones stopped me.

"Get glasses and we both take a plug", He said. That stopped my coughing.

I reached down again and opened the same drawer and took out two reasonably clean glasses. I poured full drinks.

"You're a trusting piece," I said as I handed him a glass. "I could have had a gun in that drawer".

"Why should you shoot me? You don't even know me.", he said taking the glass and raising it to toast.

What had said was odd because he could have shot me, someone he didn't know.

I raised my glass back to the bastard and we both chugged away. I resisted the impulse to the throw my empty glass at him.

"What do you charge?", he asked as he put his glass on the desk.

"Twenty-five a day and expenses", I said putting my glass down.

"Give you thirty a day, no expenses, and you got a week to find him", he said. "You need a, what you call that money up-front?"

"A retainer? Are you kidding? Not from you. I'll just take the twenty-five", I said.

"You break my heart talking like that. You make me think you scared of me or something or my money ain't no good", he said with a fake laugh. He looked at his watch and reached inside his other coat pocket. I had to fight the urge to stand up and raise my hands, but he just pulled out a wallet that would choke a cow.

He counted out money and said "Here's two-hundred-ten". Laying the cash on my desk.

He then got up and walked to the door but stopped and said over his shoulder, "Clocks running, kid. I be back in a week and you can tell me you gave him the message and set up a two-day meeting place, his choice".

"Good. When the meet is set and I inform you, then the job is over, right?"

He gave me a funny look. "Why you think that"?

"Because for me the job is done and what you guys discuss is none-of-my-business. Also, I don't want to be around for the festivities".

"Ok, I can agree with that", he said.

I said, "Thank-You".

"Thank me my ass. Thank me when it's over", He said and left.

I listened as he went down the stairs, heard the door at the bottom open and close.

I sat back in my chair, closed my eyes, and looked up to the ceiling. A part of me wanted to run after Mr. Jones and tell him I couldn't do his dirty work. But then I opened my pretty brown eyes and looked down at the new-looking twenties and a five lying innocently on my desk. I felt them, not with love but with a bit of loathing. Then I noticed the chiseler was ten-dollars short!

Whatever, came the thought.

"If I didn't need you all", I said to them new bills. "I'd throw you all out the damn window!"

All I had to do was find that bastard Renfro Jones, give him the message and run away like hell to the hills. Bad idea to be anywhere near them, I thought as I raised my head to ceiling again, tilted back my chair and closed my eyes, knowing that somebody was going to get a bullet or bullets before this was over.

Twenty minutes later I woke and dragged myself back to the here and now.

I reached in the same whiskey drawer and bought out my .38 caliber "Colt Detective". It was one of my two guns only difference being that it worked. The other was a silver-plated .45 that couldn't shoot and was for show. She was named Marylyn and was kept on top of my fridge at home. She couldn't shoot because she was filled with cement because that's how I wanted it. She was a pretty gun and was named for a pretty girl I once knew. Nice to look at and handle, the girl that I never handled.

She just couldn't laugh because she was dead.

I smiled at all this as I put the .38 in my shoulder-holster and thought that I could have shot Mr. Jones three times to his none. My .38 was just that good. Or was it just that I was that good? I thought.

The bottle of whiskey was still on my desk and I took a shot the way it should be drunk, right out of the bottle. I ignored the 2 half-filled glasses on the desk, they were not going anywhere. I put the bottle back in its cage and patted it. "The better to find you with", I said.

I got up and forced my butt, which always seemed to get lazy when I had money in my pocket, out of the office. The clock over the door said ten minutes to 6:00pm.

I had an idea where Renfro was but he would be a real fool to be there, Mr. Jones could have found him easy. I didn't know Renfro well but I did know he was no fool. So off I went to "The Avenue", as it was reverently called, to talk to some guys and maybe a few girls I would rather not talk too. Why?

Because deep down they were all my people. I was just like them, but I held back or I would be just running wild with them...and maybe enjoying it.

It was Russell Street that we called "The Avenue". It was a long street that contained all a Negro could use, or so the city planners thought, naturally not knowing a damn thing or caring about our needs. They inadvertently created, by its aim of exclusion of said Negro to use the downtown part of the city, a kind of paradise. Actually, the cities "downtown" had very little we wanted to buy in the first place.

Once we had "The Avenue", we opened our own grocery stories, butcher shops (with its weekend specials of so many pounds of meat for $25), shoe stores, grocery stores, clothes stores, liquor stores, and pool rooms. The pool-rooms had "man-sized" pool tables and if you played these tables, you'd never want to play a "pee-wee" table as they were called.

The barbers there were professionals and the "shops" were fun to visit just for the Hell of it. You got the news, gossip, and the junk-talk, of what was happening all over town, plus what was going on in the world to a point.

You also got valuable information from our spies, mostly janitors and such, in City Hall, of our illustrious politicians and most-honored leaders. Leaders who not to our surprise turned out to be not as smart as they led us to believe. "I could've done better than that!", was our popular saying when some politician made a bad decision or handled a situation flat out wrong.

I really liked Russell Street but made it a point not be there at night. It looked kinda rough in broad daylight, depending on where you looked, so I was sure that it got rougher when the Sun went down. I imagined the drug deals that went on, the use of a knife and such on seemingly innocent misunderstanding. I also had the suspicion that there were at least one or more whorehouses on the street, somewhat invisible. For instance, what was this and that house that was always was locked up tight as a drum? What was strange was that there was never talk of prostitution, either you knew where it was or you didn't. I preferred not to know.

So, I was walking down our city's busy Main Street, made my left turn to a dead still, no-city-lighted alley with long continuous brick building on either side, an alley that gave the impression of the parting of a brick sea, that lead to "The Avenue".

Actually, the street was not as loud as our Main Street because cars were not allowed on it. You still had to watch out for idiots on bikes who thought they were on a highway, otherwise the street was filled with people walking on both sidewalks of the street and in the street. There was laughter and it not unusual to see three or four people just standing in the middle of the street laughing and talking. You could also see the occasional person who talked and laughed with himself. We affectionately called these people "politicians", because they at least knew what they were talking and to whom.

I had a place in mind to go and wanted to get to it and off "The Avenue" as fast as possible, however, *The Fates* laughed at this plan and head-on there came the six-foot-three JennieLee. I had not been paying attention where I was going so there was no way to avoid her. We almost collided. Amused, she regarded me with those pretty, enticing, mesmerizing, yellow-green predator eyes.

"Well, hey there, Prince James. You *bastard*", was her greeting that was friendlier than usual. She had a way of cursing you that sounded sweet. JennieLee was not so dangerous in a physical way, she did not carry a gun, knife, icepick, or blackjack, nor would she spit on you. Her main weapon, at least against me I thought, were her eyes. I suspected her of being a witch, which was ridiculous because our television did not feature Negro witches so they did not exist. Her power over me, which was delightful and scary at the same time, was just my awkwardness with females in general.

Hey, JennieLee. How you doing?"

"I'm doing fine, Mister. How *you* doing?"

"Fine", I said and looking for a way around her. She was having none of that and stepped closer.

"You don't look fine, Negro. When the Hell you coming to see me?".

"Well, soon JennieLee, soon. I just been busy and..."

"Busy Hell and *soon* Hell, to you Sir" she said. "Both Hells together still make a big fat zero, Mister James. But what is it about you that tells me that you act like a married man. You married, Sir?".

"No. What gave you *that* idea?", I said.

"The way you act Mr. James. So, you ain't married and you ain't no Preacher." she said moving face to face. "So, what is it that keeps you from going *wild*, Brother dear, unlike the other Brothers?", she asked with those now glowing eyes.

"I don't know, I guess I'm just trying keep my cool and not go ballistic, or something…"

She gave me short gentle kiss on the lips and said "Well, ballistic *is* a nice thought. Though unrealized in such as you. Well, Brother-dear, you just come by anytime, ballistic or not, and I show you how to hurt *and* get wild. I know you understand me cause you smarter than you act. Just one more thing though", she said.

"What's....that", I said.

She patted my cheek. "Don't take too long, Brother", she said and walked around me.

I stood there for a long moment and noted that some guys and sisters where walking by me with knowing smiles. Mentally I shook off JennieLee as best I could. I did not want to be just standing in the street looking like a politician.

I made my way to one of the pool rooms, actually "the" pool room on the avenue, "Fat Sally's", with its so-called "ten-footer" pool tables, and very little smoke in the air though you were allowed to smoke. You shot by "challenge", all you had to do was put your quarter on the railing in line with the other quarters and waited your turn. If you didn't wait your turn, you might get a pool-stick to the head, or so I heard. I came in out of a darkening sky to a well-lit room full of guys talking, laughing, joking, sulking, smoking, and lastly, shooting pool. Some were doing these things all that at once.

I walked and saw an empty table at the back and made my way to it, going around the shooters and crap talkers. Some of them nodded at me as did a few sittings on benches drinking beer. I knew that some of the beer bottles contained something else. Before I got to the last table, which was not used and reserved for "Fat Sally", I looked up to see the walled-up office with its one-way mirror looking out over the empire. There were stairs going up to it but I didn't get that far. A really big joker, big as a grizzly, blocked my way, seeming to come from nowhere.

"What you want?", he said sounding like a grizzly but not quite. Didn't matter. He was big enough to sound any way he wanted.

"Big Sally here?", I asked, trying to sound cool. He was not impressed.

"Big Sally sent for you mug?", pushing down his big face and big eyes at me.

I didn't like the "mug" shot so I pushed my face and little eyes back up at him. "Nope, he did not send for me. We pals", I said.

That didn't impress him either.

I didn't get a chance to do anything else because he put his big paws on my shoulders and raising his voice, "He didn't call you; you don't go up. Play pool or skip to the lou out. Thems your choices".

"Look, Papa Bear, tell him I'm here and I'm going up either way!", I said.

That was it, I thought. Mr. Papa Bear stood up to his six-foot six and was preparing to throw me through the ceiling when a voice from came from above.

"It's ok Winnie, let him up. You can always kill him later", came the manly vocal of Big Sally. I was saved.

We both turned our heads up to see him standing on the landing at the top of the stairs. He waved to me.

Winnie looked back to me. I looked to him as innocently as I could.

"You lucky, Mister what-ever-the-Hell-your-name-is. Get on up there, before I change my mind!"

I got on up there as fast as dignity and bravado would let me. I looked down to see a frowning Winnie and decided not to leave by way of him. I also noticed everybody else was still playing pool, minding their own business.

Since the door was shut, I knocked. A voice said "In!".

I came in an office with a desk and chair in back of it and "Sally", whose real name was Hubo Jenkins sitting behind the desk. He gave me the once over and gave a nod that was not for me, but a signal for two guys, obviously related to Winnie at least by their size, appearing suddenly to the left and right of me.

"Get em up", one said. Which I did while another guy began

frisking me. The first guy took off my hat and looked in as if for a grenade, handed it back to me and said "Clean". The second guy said, "Clean".

The three of us were now looking at Hubo.

"So which way is the cow flying, Mr. James?", Hubo asked.

Confused, the searchers looked at each other but I knew what Hubo meant.

"She be flying the right way, I said. "I just need to ask you something".

Hubo smiled. "Good to see you, so ask away. I got no secrets from these guys.

"In that case, I'll be on my way". I turned to walk away. The two guys blocked me.

"That hat?", Hubo said.

Over my shoulder I said, "Yeah, that's hat".

Silence.

Then, "Get downstairs boys, close the door on your way out".

Both guys turned to look at Hubo, then at me. Neither liked the play.

"It's alright, partners. I know this guy", Hubo said.

They left but not happy about it.

I sat. "Hubo", I said.

"Mr. Frigging A. James, what the Hell you want?"

"Hubo. I'm on a job that's got nothing to do with you, but I need to know where Renfro is".

He stood up. Angry.

"He's, my cousin. You know that so you best tell me what you want him for", he said now pacing back and forth behind the desk.

"The job's clean, no danger for Renfro, all I have to do is give him a message, and go home. That's it", I said.

"That's it? Sounds too simple, Man. So, what's the message?", he asked still pacing.

"I can't tell you, Hubo and you know that. It's just business".

He stopped pacing. "Business my ass! Either tell me our get out...through the front-door!"

"Ok, look, you know what I do for a living. But since we know each other, I'll tell you part of it. I have to deliver the message to Renfro in a week. Also, you can be with us both when I deliver the whole message", I lied.

Silence.

"Come on, man, you know that I wouldn't pull nothing on Renfro or you.", I said.

He studied me, then sat down. "Ok", he said, "But who you working for"?

"Can't tell you that, even if I knew his real name".

"Get real! You took a job and don't know who you working for!"

"Well, I do have a name, but I'm ninety percent sure it's fake. I'll give to you and Renfro when we meet. then you both on your own!", I said.

He stopped pacing and went back to his desk. He reached down and opened a drawer and I had just a second to hope that I wouldn't be looking at another gun in the face. No gun crawled out, but what he did pull out was just as bad.

He pulled his Scotch. I hate Scotch and Hubo knew it.

He just smiled and handed me the bottle which reminded me of a jug, so heavy it was.

"Damn", I said.

I opened the bottle and took a shot and handed it back to him. He took a longer shot that turned into a chug, put the bottle down and made a contented sigh.

"I love insulting expensive liquor!", he said with a grin and got serious. "I don't know where he is, but I'll can Ren and set up a meet. That's all I can do since you won't or can't tell me what's going on! You got that?"

"I got ears, don't I", I said, reaching for that horrible stuff and taking another shot.

"No slip-ups, Brother James. Make sure you take care of your end and you ain't followed or something. It won't matter if you don't know if something went wrong. We will come after you just the same", Hubo said as he grabbed the bottle again and drank. "No hard feelings if it comes to that. Ok?".

"Ok. No hard feeling but the guy I'm working for...I don't trust him. Reminds me of a snake".

He gave me the somber look of alcohol induced insight. "He probably is a snake or something worse, but he's *your* end Brother. If he's crosses you, then you take em out, and I don't mean to dinner, OR, let me know, IF you can, then we'll take him out".

"OK!", I said. The damn Scotch was working "Guess that will make me rest easier in my grave!".

Hubo gave me a strange look and said, "Now that's smart and true. Now, what's that part again you can't tell me?"

"Hey, hey, hey, I already *told* you at least *one* part that I had no business telling you anyway, Mister Hubo! One part too many!", I fairly flounced.

"Awwwwww, come ON, MAN! Gimme something else to chew on!".

"Chew on! *Chew* on? Good God!", I said, rolling my eyes to a sky that I swore I could see.

"He, my gracious and generous bastard client, or is it client bastard? ... told *me* that *your* Renfro took three of his girls. You know anything about that?"

I was just fishing for information but Hubo, normally a cool dude, froze as if he'd been struck on the ear by a bb-gun pellet or something. He recovered quickly. I sobered up a bit.

"Nope", he replied mustering his cool. "I don't know a thing about that. You spy a tail on your way here?" Trying to change the subject.

"Damn", I said surprised. "If I was followed? Man, I didn't even think to look".

"Some detective you are".

"Yeah, you know it. I been thinking about quitting my de-tec-tive work and run for President or Kaiser or something", I said as I started to get up to leave. I was anxious to get out of there.

"You and me both, Bro! By the way, how's JennieLee doing these days?", he said, an all-knowing smirk on his face. He knew that JennieLee was my needle and he liked sticking me in the eye with it. The bastard.

"JennieLee, as far as *I* know, is doing fine, Man, and you know she is", I said sitting back down, the alcohol pushing me further down. My butt was psychologically trying to find the floor.

"By the way", I said, "How's Grandma Jones doing? She might know where Renfro is and…"

"Best you leave Grandma Jones out of this, James", he said getting serious again. He always could hold his liquor better than me. "She'd cut your nose off as look at you and especially if you stuck it in family business. That's good advice from me, a Scotch drinker, straight and true!"

"Ok, sorry", I said but not sorry at all. It was getting strange in here.

"You know, like I was saying before you asking about Grandma, I always had a *thing* for JennieLee". His eyes went out of focus and I know he was seeing her floating in room or something.

"Why don't you put in a good word for me, James?", he said and all the mirth was gone. He was serious.

"You couldn't handle her, Hubo. I think she's a witch", I said.

"They all witches as far as I know, but I don't care about that! She can put a spell on me anytime!", he said.

It got quiet. We both looking at each other when suddenly we both burst out laughing our heads off. It lasted for while then stopped. We both shaking our heads.

"Why don't you go to Hell?", I said.

"Yeah, you right. Why don't we both go to Hell", he said with a melancholy that scared me. Time to split.

"Is there a back-way out of here?", I asked as I hauled myself up.

"Yeah. Why?" he said looking somewhere over my head.

"Because a lot of people saw me come in here. I don't want them to see me go out. They might get curious or…"

"Something?", he said with a grin. "I'll take you out myself and it'll look like I got sore. Most people know the back-door out is bad-news. Let's go", he said and now we both were up.

Hubo took me out in such a way that I would never be able to find my way back in. There were a lot of turns and twists. Once we went down a long set of concrete stairs just to come back up a longer set of metal stairs. On that landing I could hear pool being played and I thought we had somehow doubled back. But I was wrong. Hubo opened a huge metal door that a bank would have been proud of, I just had time to look at an ugly smile as the bastard pushed me out in a dark alley.

I started walking. It was so dark that I could barely see my hand in front of my face. I stepped on a body. The body didn't seem to mind so I walked faster, made a turn, and finally saw a lighted cross-street ahead. I made it to that cross-street and had no idea where I was and since that was so, I just played Columbus and turned right. I walked five blocks on a street where every third street-light was on, but dim. In-between the lights were just dark buildings, on each side the street, facing an even darker side-walk. Suddenly, I had the feeling I was being followed so I stopped in a lighted area, which was not a good idea. Realizing that, I speeded up my walk and stopped in a dark section of side-walk and listened. Sure enough, I heard two foot-steps behind me that had stopped too late.

I looked back, but all there was where lighted areas with dark between them as far as I could see. I thought I was hidden well but then realized that I was actually half-in and half-out of a street-lighted area. My follower could see me, so I took off to the next corner and made another right turn. No street-lights at all just darkness, but I could see, one or two blocks in the distance, Manna from Heaven! A liquor store, lit-up like a Christmas tree which meant it was open!

I ran to it and was almost out of breath when I went in, barely having time to notice the sign, "Harry T.C. Schofield, Proprietor, and "If you drink it, we got it. **No Credit**", on the door.

There seemed to be nobody home.

"Hello!", I yelled.

"Hello yourself", came a deep voice from the ceiling. I looked up to a friendly faced man on a ladder about six-feet up, a bottle in each hand. He turned and placed one on a shelf.

"Just a minute", he said as he came down one-rung and placed another bottle, that looked like expensive whiskey, on another shelf. He started down.

I walked to the front-counter, making a show of placing both my hands on that same counter so he could see them. I didn't want any misunderstanding.

He got to the bottom and we faced each other. He was a tall, old guy with dark-grey eyes. He was going bald, thinning hair on each side of small-eared face. He was clean shaven, no mustache, but he had a small round ear-ring is his right-ear. He was smiling at me with good teeth but what put me off was a scar from the bottom of his left-eye that disappeared under his shirt.

"I'm glad to see you. Are you Mr. Schofield?", I asked him.

"I'm glad to see you too, Sir, and you right as rain, I'm the owner. Customers are always welcome. No matter the time. So, what'll it be…friend?", he said with a whimsical smile.

"Well,", I said, "Er, now that you ask, I got a taste for vodka tonight and...", I turned to look through the glass-door I came in, but all I saw was a facing street that was lit like the others behind me. Nothing moved.

"You in some kind of trouble, Son?", he said.

I turned at the word "Son". Nobody had called me that in a long, long, time. Not since...

"No, Sir. None at all", I finally said.

"That's good and if there were, I could handle it for you" He reached under the counter and patted something. I bet it was a gun and, in his business, it had to be a gun that worked.

"Good", I said. "I'll take a bottle of "Nikki's Prudence", please".

The man grimaced." Good Grief, you *drink* that stuff? They don't make much of it these days. I used to think Nikki has lost her Prudence down holes to kill rats! You sure that's what you want?", he said chuckling away.

"Yes, Sir", I said. He hunched his shoulders and with another chuckle started back up the ladder. "What time is it? It seems to be late as heck".

"Oh, it's no later than 9:00pm", he said as he went up.

"It seems later because it gets darker around here sooner because the city is trying the save money on the damn street-lights", He said. "Bunch of lazy bastards, if you ask me. Bet whatever they save they put in their own pockets".

"Oh, I bet that's true", I said. Looking up to him as he reached for the bottle of *Nikki's Prudence 85 Proof, Green Label*, the bottler's only label.

"Yep, I know some of them by name and some them by smell", he said as he came down with the bottle.

"Well, what can you do the way things are set up. You can't get the bastards out of office, they stay in till they die", I said looking up at him.

That elicited a laugh as Mr. Schofield came down and I was about to say more when at least three shots went right over my head! At least one of them seem to go by ear like a mosquito going 1000

miles-an-hour. I swear I watched two bullets that blossomed red in Mr. Schofield's back and one missing him hitting a bottle a bit above him. Smelled like Scotch from where I stood.

Mr. Schofield miraculously held on to my *Nikki* as he came down and placed her on a back-counter in front of him. Then he just folded, fell from ladder hitting his head on that same counter to the floor. While all of this happened, I just froze. Whoever was shooting had me in their sights and had all day to shoot me. That meant the shooter was not after me.

I leaned over the counter to look at Mr. Schofield, but all I got in my face was a bunch of teeth from the biggest dog I've ever seen. He was cream-colored and had to be 5 feet long. I leaned back from the counter and the dog, both front paws now placed on the counter, leaned back with me snarling and snapping his jaws.

"Easy boy, eeeeeasy now", I whispered to him, fighting my desire to take off to the door. But I would have never made it anyway and I did not want to do anything to provoke this so-called dog.

"Easy boy, easy now. I was already in here, you know that. You know I didn't shoot him. Don't you boy? You heard us talking, right? Yes, you did", I said trying to be friendly. "Easy, now".

This sweet talk calmed him a little, but he pulled himself up on the counter on all four-legs and had the whitest teeth I've ever seen as he now just snapping his jaws at me, ears back, eyes open wide.

I had to do something and quick. No way I was going to just stand there and talk to a dog that might misunderstand me at any second and attack. I got an idea.

I raised a palm and started backing slowly to the door. The effect was instant.

The animal stopped snapping and lowered his head to glare at me and it was then I saw that it had only one-eye, one squinting black eye, the other missing. As I backed to the front-door, it jumped from counter to floor like some big cat and following me.

"Yeah, that's good, that's a good dog..."

I guess "good dog" was the wrong thing to say, because he stopped and was snarling again.

"Sorry, sorry. I didn't mean that.... easy now", as I backed up and kept eye to eye contact. He followed. We were close to the front-door when he suddenly stopped, stiff-legged. I froze.

His eye locked on something over my shoulder, through the glass-door, and up the facing street. Somewhere in that darkness he was seeing something.

Cautiously, I felt for the door-handle getting lucky and opening it slowly inside, standing there like a doorman waiting for a customer to go out. The dog's head and eye came down to look at me. No longer snarling he seemed to waiting for me to do something.

So, I whispered", "*Get him boy*, get him. *Go get him!*".

He looked from me to that facing street, then back to me, inclined his big head one way and then the other as if conflicted, confused.

Then I got it, but it could just as easy work on me. With a bravado I really did not feel, I opened the door wider and said all at once, loudly now, "*Sickem* boy! Go get the *bastard,* yeah! GO!"

The dog charged by me so fast I barely had time to see the end of its tail go by. I looked up to see him bound up the street, then wheeling to the left-side into the darkness.

Letting out a long breath and getting my heartbeat under control, I closed and locked the door and ran behind the counter. Mr. Schofield was laying on his right-side, facing the back-counter, his legs askew. I didn't see much blood but I smelled something. I started to place my fingers on his throat for a pulse, but why? It was death that I smelled, not blood.

I turned to look for a phone and found it, black and impersonal as usual, under the front-counter, next to a sawed-off shotgun and a .45 pistol that looked military-issue.

I placed the phone on the counter and dialed the police. Oddly enough, they answered after the first ring.

"Police Department. Officer Dodd".

"Really", I said.

"What's that", came the reply from Officer Dodd.

"A man's been shoot in his liquor store", I said.

"In *his* liquor store? You mean the owner"?

"Yes, I do, Officer Dodd", I said.

"Address"?

"By the card I see here its....1313 Friday Lane".

"Friday Lane", he said and paused.

"Yep", I said with relish ignoring his pause, realizing from his tone that cops in general didn't like responding to calls from this particular street. I could sympathize with him.

"Your name?", asked Officer Dodd

"Milton James, Private Eye, First-Class. Owner's name is Harry T. C. Schofield".

"I'm sure. Wonderful, wonderful. Well, Mr. "First-Class, I'll send over two cars of our finest to assist you. Don't touch anything", he said.

"Will you be attending, Officer Dodd?", I asked him innocently.

Another pause.

"Regrettably, I have other duties to perform that will allow me to keep my head where it is. You sit tight".

"Oh, be sure to send an ambulance over. I think Mr. Schofield's dead.", I said.

Another pause.

"Of course. Wonderful. Keeps getting better and better by the minute. Sit tight!", he said.

I hung up and put the phone on top of the counter. I was sure it, and its friends down-under, would not miss each other.

I then went to the other side of the counter and tried to *sit tight* standing up.

It was no more 20 minutes when I heard the sirens coming. Yep, like the cavalry, our police were coming with a lot noise in the late evening, noise enough to hopefully scare away any crime going on so they wouldn't have more trouble to deal with.

One car came from the left, the other from the right, and I watched in comic relief as they skidded to a stop almost colliding head-on. Four uniformed policemen got out and ran in, single file. Well done I thought to myself. I then saw a plain car pull up silently from the left.

The first officer came me, right up to me, stopped, and looked around. Seeing no murder, since it wasn't me, so he asked, "Ok Mister, where is he?"

"Other side of the counter", I said.

"Ok, I'll go", he said but only made one step.

"Leave it Sergeant Kilbourne!", came a loud voice from the front-door. Two men from the third car, in very plain clothes, came in. The one who gave the order was the 13th Precinct Police Lieutenant Harvey Miller followed by Richard Lee (Lefty) Maroni, his underling who was actually right-handed.

"I'll take over. You and your partner wait outside and keep the curious away", Lieutenant Miller ordered.

The Sergeant didn't like that. With a frown he said to his fellows, "Come on Officers. Take your positions outside, like the Lieutenant says". The Sergeant, still frowning and now mumbling, herded the Officers outside and stationed two on each side of the front-door.

"Lefty, take a look.", Lieutenant Miller said.

Lefty walked around me not giving me a glance, stopped at the counter, looked over and went around to the man.

"Guy seems to be dead Lieutenant. Strange, not a lot of blood here", Lefty said.

"I'll bet, but just wait till we move him", the Lieutenant said, giving me a funny look to which I shook my head for him to wait. He gave me a "are you kidding look?" and I shook my head again. Lefty came back to us.

Just then the front door was opened by Sergeant Kilbourne who said, "There a *big* dog coming from up the street. Looks like he want's in".

I said quickly, "Let him in Sergeant, please, don't you or the other Officers go for their guns. Dog's very dangerous".

"Dangerous?", Sergeant Kilbourne said.

"Yeah. The dead man is its master. The dog is...well, angry. Just let him in and stay out of his way", I answered.

The Sergeant stepped back leaving the door open. I could see him outside briefing the group and saw when they all, two on each side of the door, recoil. They all stepped back from the door even further, having all seeing something they didn't like. The dog came through the door and in to the light.

The dog's head, from its muzzle to down below its neck and from the top his head, half way back along its spine was covered with wet, glistening blood. We took a step back. Lefty started to reach inside his coat but I slowly raised a palm to him and he stopped. The whole time the dog ignored us as it walked slowly by, then jumped on top of the counter, looked back at us and jumped down to his master.

We three gave each other looks. Sergeant Kilbourne peered in and Lefty said, "We're fine, Sergeant. Don't let anybody else in here except the Doc and ambulance. Close the door, please".

The Sergeant closed the door and we tip-toed, like rats on two-legs, and looked over the counter.

The dog was lying next to its Master. The blood on it now on its master. The dog looked up at us with its one-eye, big head, and sad expression, and laid its head down on the dead man's arm, snuggling its body to the man's back.

We walked back to the front-door.

"Damn, that's a really big dog. Never seen anything like that. What the Hell…?", Harvey said.

"Irish Wolfhound", came the quick answer from Lefty.

We turned to him.

"How you know that?", I asked, surprised he would know.

"Well, I have a dog at home myself. Small one. Nothing *that* big. My Uncle lives up-state and we had a dog just like that when I was little. I used to ride him", Lefty said.

"*Ride him!* You mean…like a horse?", Lieutenant Miller asked.

"Yep", came the answer from Lefty.

"Are they vicious?", Harvey asked. "Gosh, I bet they are, and I bet it won't let anybody get near the body!" Harvey said pointing toward the counter.

"Nawww, they ain't vicious as a rule. This one's kind of small, Its female. Looks to be, 150 pounds. Could go to 180 easy. Usually a nice, friendly dog. I used to play with my Uncle's which was male, 200 pounds of fun…", Lefty said as if looking back in his past. He snapped out of it and said to the Lieutenant, "But right now in the state it's in, I wouldn't go near it".

"Ok, ok, wonderful. Female you say? How you know that?", the Lieutenant asked.

"Noticed as she went by, Lieutenant", Lefty replied, giving me a wink that the Lieutenant did not see.

"Oh. Wonderful, just wonderful. Lefty, go to the car-radio and find out where's the Doc", Harvey ordered.

Lefty didn't seem to have heard. His attention was on the counter.

"Lefty?", Harvey said.

Lefty looked at Harvey and said, "Sure Lieutenant. Thanks".

Harvey gave Lefty a funny look, then the same to me. I just hunched my shoulder. We watched Lefty as he went out, the four Officers watching him as if for ordered, and got in the car.

"What the *Hell* is going on in here! This confusion looks like some of *your* work, James! Is all this part of something you working on!", he asked with a tense low voice.

"No, no, no! Absolutely not! This ain't got nothing to do with me and I don't have time for it. I need leave, Harve", I pleaded.

"You know you just can't walk away from a murder! Especially one *you* called in! Are you nuts! And don't call me *Harve* he said. "You know I don't like it!"

"I'm not nuts! Look, I just talked to a guy who is a friend of the guy I'm looking for. We got kinda drunk and he let me out on a street that I've never been on before. I got lost and the more I wondered around, the more I got lost. Then I noticed someone was following me and got lucky and found this store. I was talking with guy and next thing I know the guy gets shot. Not my fault, Harve".

"Really? Not your fault? Ok, I'll bite. How many shots", Harvey said.

"Three. At least three, one of which went right by *this* ear", I replied pointing to my right-ear.

"In any case, the Captain will want to talk to you so get ready for that, Mister James"

"Don't care about your damn Captain and you know that, but there's something you need to know."

"And what is that, Mister. James", Harvey said as Lefty came in.

"After the shooting was over, I wanted to take a look at the guy but dog won't let me, so I let her out and she did a strange thing", I said.

"Like what? Lefty asked.

She ran out, straight up the street there out of sight", I said pointing up the facing street.

I could see Lefty was thinking about that. "How fast?", he asked.

"Really fast", I said.

"Was she barking or bellowing or something?", Lefty asked.

"Nope. Just out like a streak up that street", I said.

Harvey was getting impatient and said quickly, "What's this go to do with anything, Lefty?"

"Maybe nothing, Lieutenant, but I think we should search that street, Sir".

Lefty had never called the Lieutenant "Sir", to my knowledge, so that got his attention.

"Ok, I get it. You think maybe the dog was maybe after the

shooter?", Harvey asked.

"Yeah. Or maybe after whoever she could find up there", Lefty said.

That was it. Harvey motioned me to stay where I was, and motioned Lefty to follow him. They both went out and corralled the two uniformed officers. Harvey got them in a group and pointed up the facing street and the two uniformed and Lefty ran up the street. I could see them split up to search both sides of the street. Harvey turned to come back in.

It was all getting on my nerves. I had a case to work but couldn't, so I reached for relief and took the bottle of Nikki's, screwed her open and took a good shot.

Harvey came in. Closed the door and gave me his best disapproval look and said to me during

My mid-gurgle, "Good Grief, couldn't wait could you!"

I finished and said, "No, I couldn't Lieutenant. That was really good!". I offered him a shot but he shook his head.

I looked at the bottle and reached for my wallet. I had not paid for the liquor. I took out a

ten-dollar bill and put it the cash register. Then I toasted Mr. Schofield and took another shot.

Harvey just stared.

I was on my third shot when the ambulance rolled up fast, no siren but with red-lights flashing and double-parking next to Harvey's car. Two guys unloaded a stretcher as Doctor Homer S. Ladder came in. Everybody knew he was sensitive about his name, and "get a Ladder" was the common phase he hated, so we were just called him Doc. I secured my bottle. Doc did not approve of alcohol as I did, just in time to put a finger to my lips for quiet. He thought I was crazy.

"What Hell you doing that for?", Doc said?

The other two guys came in with their noise and their stretcher, but stopped cold when they heard an ominous growl behind the counter. I gave them the same warning I gave Doc.

"I don't do animal-calls. Is this some kind of joke, *Mister James?*", the Doc said putout.

"No, Doc this is no kind a joke. There's a guy over the counter been shot twice and one of the biggest dogs I'm ever seen. The animal won't let anyone near the body", I said.

"Oh, Hell! We don't have time for this. You sure about this dog business? Why don't you guys just shoot the bastard", Doc said.

"Well yeah, we're sure about the dog and nobody thought of shooting the poor thing. I'm sure the SPCA* would object", I said.

We all just stood around for a moment until one of the medics said, "I think I can help. I got an idea".

*Society for the Prevention of Cruelty to Animal

"Idea? Hope it's a good one. Dog's an Irish Wolfhound. *Big*", I said.

"Whoa! That don't sound to good, Harry, and outside the call of duty", The other medic said.

"Sam, what else can we do. You got a solution?", Harry said and looked to the Doc

"SPCA Hell! Well, whatever you got just be careful", Doc said.

"Being careful is on my mind all the time, Doc. You all be quiet and wait", Harry said.

Harry closed his eyes, opened them, and walked slowly to the counter mouthing in a whisper a language I'd never heard.

"Shinn-go-na, Shinn-go-na, Lo-bee-to, Lo-bee-to. Shinn-go-na so, Lo-bee-to", Harry intoned.

There was a low growl behind the counter.

"Lo-bee-ta, Lo-bee-to, Lo-bee-to. Roooo-na-ooooo, Roooo-na-ooooo, Yo Lo-bee-to, Lo-bee-to".

There was another growl that turned to a low whine.

Harry was at the counter now, had to see the dog and the dog seeing him for sure. He repeated his words. The room went still and my eyes fluttered and began to drupe. Harvey nudged me but it didn't help. I was going under.

"Shoko bee to, me Lo-bee to, No-che-mino, No-che-mino", Harry said soothingly.

If anyone came in right then, they would have seen the four of us stock-still in place, eyes half-closed. I managed to open my eyes and looked down to see the Doc holding me up, one arm under my arm. I said in a whisper, "Guys". That was enough for the Doc, Harvey, Sam and me to get back to a real world.

Harry studied the dog a few moments more, then looked back at us satisfied and went around the counter. Harvey put his hand in his coat for his weapon. I gave him my best "Are *you* crazy look?" but his hand stayed inside on his service-revolver, waiting.

Harry could be seen bending down then come up grimacing with the dog in his arms. He came around the counter quickly and went out the front-door that Harvey opened, keeping as much distance between the two as could. Sam followed them out.

We saw Harry carrying his load to the ambulance. Sam ran ahead of him and opened both the ambulance's back-doors and hopped-in.

He turned around just in time to help Harry bring the dog in. Both guys assisted each other to lay the dog down gently. Then they came back to us.

"Whew! That's a heavy dog!", Harry said.

"What Hell was that singing?", Doc asked.

"Oh, I use that on my newborn at home. Puts her to sleep. I guess the dog will be out of it for at least four hours", Harry said.

"Damn good work, Harry! Now let's get to it!", Doc said and went around the counter to make his examination.

Harvey, Sam, Harry and I were now looking over the counter while the Doc worked.

"Well, man's dead. I see...two high-caliber bullet wounds in his back, not much blood on his shirt but both wounds high enough to do his heart no good," Doc said. He turned the man over.

"That's strange. No exit wounds in the front".

"Why strange, Doc", Harvey said.

"It's just that...", Doc began but unbuttoned the man's shirt all the way to the belt. "A-ha!", he said. "Bullet proof vest!".

Harvey gave me a quizzical look as if I had had something to do that. I ignored him.

"Why the bullet-proof vest?", Harvey asked.

"Good question. Well, this is a tough part of town but not a war-zone. I suspect a damn lot of guns was used on him. The vest is somewhat vintage, not made to take the kind of bullet he got", Doc replied.

"Why you say that, Doc?", I asked and gave Harvey his quizzical look back. He didn't like it.

"Seen a lot of bullet-proof vests in my time", Doc said. "In the war and about. Most of them don't live up to their damn name. Some are good, most are downright useless. All I can say is that the thing he's wearing is not a military vest.

I bet no exit-wounds because the body must have slowed the bullets down, or maybe both hit a rib or something, enough so that they just stayed in the body…or whatever. I'll let you guys know more when I get him on the table tomorrow".

"Why tomorrow, Doc? Why not tonight?", Harvey asked.

"Oh, he'll keep till tomorrow. I need to get my dinner", Doc laughed, motioning to Harry and Sam. "You guys take him and watch out for that damn dog. Don't need two more patients", he joked.

Harry and Sam took the stretcher around the counter and loaded the dead man. They were close to the front-door when Officer Joe came running in, out of breath and out of color.

"Doc, he said, there's another dead guy up the street, throat's been....". That was as far as he got as his eyes bulged and he ran back outside and vomited.

"Go on and put him in the wagon, boys", Harvey said.

Harry and Sam went out pass Officer Joe, who was still bent over retching but seemed to be recovering. The Doc could be seen walking up the street. He stopped briefly to talk with Lefty who was coming down. Lefty turned and pointed to an area on the left-side of street, between two building. Doc turned that way and Lefty came on.

"What that's all about?", Harvey said after watching them. "I got a feeling you mixed in this some kind of way James".

I had nothing at all to add to that so I kept my mouth shut. We both looked up the street, watching Lefty come down in a slow melancholy way.

"Taking his sweet time, ain't he?", I said.

"Must be really bad up there", Harvey said as the ambulance speeded by, red-lights flashing but no siren, ominous and final.

Lefty walked in. Looked at me, then at Harvey who said, "Well?".

"Whew. There's a man up there got his throat wide open. Almost relieved head from body. Blood everywhere. Seems to be a lot of God-damn blood around here tonight. Too much damn blood," Lefty said.

"Steady, Lefty", I said. "Ain't that bad. You can handle it. It's just part of your job", I said.

Harvey stared at me. Lefty stared at me.

"Save your anger for something more serious, something you'll probably never see. The bastard you up there don't deserve no sympathy from nobody", I said.

"Why you say that?", Lefty said.

Harvey interrupted and said, "He means that guy was just a criminal. Worse, a paid murderer. You found a weapon that was used to kill a man tonight. Am I correct, *Officer*?", Harvey asked.

"Well, yeah. Good looking rifle...a killing machine, scope and all. Professional, bet you could kill an elephant with that thing",

Lefty said.

"To Hell with him then. Son of a Bitch, lowdown dirty Mother got what they all get in the business of killing", I said looking over at Harvey. Up till then me and Lefty didn't get along at all, but I was getting the feeling that maybe in the future we could get along a bit better.

Harvey helped me by saying "Yeah, to Hell with him and every bastard lowlife CC like him!".

Just then the Doc came in, stopped and looked at the three of us. "Am I breaking up a party or something here?", he mused.

"No", Lefty said. "Just a professional discussion. Phones over their Doc", he said pointing to the black phone on the counter.

"Thanks", Doc said. "Guy's been attacked by an animal. Our dog-friend I would imagine. Never seen anything like that", he said walking over the phone where he dialed and ordered another ambulance.

"Well,", I said breezily, I guess that's those buddies! I'm going home", reaching for my bag of bottled booze and moving to the door all at once.

Harvey grabbed my arm, stopping me cold. "Hold on there, *buddy*! What's the rush, the party is just getting started!

"Lieutenant, I got work to do and this action here is just some kind of happening, not in my cards. I don't have time for it and it ain't paying my rent", I said, gently pulling my arm from his grasp.

For a few seconds we stood almost toe to toe until Lefty cleared his throat. We turned our attention to Lefty and the Lieutenant stepped back.

"Alright, Mister Detective James", the Lieutenant said. "You can go now and the Department thanks you for phoning in this most interesting *happening*."

"No problem", I said.

"But, make sure you get your butt to the station *early* in the morning to make a statement. Got that?"

"Sure, I got it Lieutenant. Won't miss it for the world", I replied turning to leave.

"And don't leave town!", the Lieutenant screamed.

I nodded to Lefty. He nodded back. Then I was moving and thought why anyone would want to leave such an exciting town.

Next morning, I flew or sailed down to the station. I don't know which one because I was so tired that my old heap just took over since she knew the way. The next thing I knew I was not only in front of the station but was guided to a legal, empty parking spot, something unheard of. I flowed out of my car like smoke and up the stairs to the Desk Sergeant who was busy, as usual, writing something and of course ignoring whoever, meaning me at this point, needed to talk to him. I noted his nametag. It woke me up.

He was sitting up, like a person on high, at his podium-style desk that surrounded him like a curved caramel, busy with the paperwork that all Desk Sergeants seems to be perpetually busy with.

"Good morning, Officer Dodd", I said brightly.

"Ain't it though", Officer Dodd replied somberly not looking up from his writing.

"Yes, it is. I'm the guy you told to "sit-tight" last night at the liquor store murder", I said.

He stopped writing, looked up, therefore down at me then looked down and his resumed his precious writing. "So, what you want me to do?", he said.

"Well,", I said raising my voice. "Since I be a taxpayer and thus be paying some of your salary, I'd like you to stop what you're doing, please, and be so kind as to tell me where Lieutenant Miller's office is. I was ordered by the Lieutenant, who responded to the murder, to come in here at this *very* inconvenient time to make same statement, Sir!"

First, I noticed Officer Dodd stopped writing, was actually listening to me, looking full-blown down at me with his narrowed grey eyes that sought to intimidate. I despise most grey-eyed anything's, so he had as much chance of scaring *me* as a red-rubber band.

Second, I noticed that the whole station; plain-clothes detectives, uniformed officers, and suspected criminals, including some rather interesting ladies of the night, had their full attention on me and Officer Dodd. I think the "taxpayer" line had done the trick but who knows. The way they looked at me you'd think I had just insulted their Mother.

Officer Dodd put his mighty pencil down, which seemed to enhance the room's quiet astonishment with a growing anticipation.

"Ok, *sir*. You need to see our one and *only* LIEU-tenant Miller?", Officer Dodd said with a breath that was surprising pleasant. I would have never guessed.

"That was the idea, Officer Dodd", I said innocently

Officer Dodd stood up from his desk, drawing himself slowly up and looking down on me as if I was trying to get into Heaven or something. I also imagined his voice was about to change as pushed his lips out and filled his cheeks with air. But to our surprise all that came out was polite sarcasm.

"Wonderful", he said, sticking out his left-arm and fingering his left.

"Be so kind as to just walk straight ahead, second right, then left, first office on your right. Think you can do that, *Sir*, or should I *escort* you?", Officer Dodd said

"Thank-You, but no escort needed or required, please", I said and walked through staring people on both sides of the department, much like parting a river or something.

Finding the Lieutenant's Office was easy. I knocked once on the door, not waiting for an answer and just walked in. To my surprise Lefty was there sitting on the edge of a desk.

"Good Morning", I said.

"Good Morning, yourself. Kind of early ain't ya?", Lefty said. "The Lieutenant won't be in for at least for two hours".

I groaned. "He told me to come in here early to…"

"Yeah, I know. But nobody believed that", Lefty said.

"I believed it!"

"Just as well you did", he said getting up and grabbing some pencils and paper. He pointed to an empty desk and chair. "Take a seat, please. Captain Samuel T. G. Winters wants a statement from you. Stay right here till I come back. I'll go look for him", he said as he walked out the door.

"Great", I groaned again and sat down to write.

Twenty minutes later Lefty came in as I finishing up. He watched me as I proofed-read it, signed it and gave it to him with grin.

He took it and said, "Sit tight", a term that seemed popular with the Police. He went out again.

I closed my eyes and actually napped a bit until Lefty gave me a gentle shake.

I awoke to the nightmare face of the most famous Captain Samuel T. J. Winters with his big grey eyes one of which larger than the other, a nose that needed work because it was too big as were his bulging jowls, a mustache that went all the way to his chin, and uneven hair cut with a bald spot a mile wide. Add to that that he not an old guy.

The Captain and I just did not get along. It could have been his grey eyes; I despise people with grey eyes. That all started with a guy whose grey-eyed actions almost got me killed, however, I think the fact Captail and I couldn't stand each other was *both* our faults, though I was sure it was mostly *his* fault...although I did like to *needle* him to a point. That point was reached when his face got awful red and *Gosh...I really enjoyed that*! What a spectacle he made of himself with those cheap-looking, round-lensed glasses he wore...

But yes, I was just as guilty. He slammed my statement down in front of me and took the chair at my desk. Lefty moved over to the other desk, took a chair, and faced us. Wonderful, I thought. Exactly what I don't like. Two cops in a room and *me* in the middle. I keep a straight face and shut mouth.

"*Well*, Mr. James?", the Captain said pushing his pretty face close to mine.

"Well, what, Captain?", I said as sweet and not giving a damn as I could.

"Is there something *else* you would like to add to your bull-shit statement?", he said pointing down to my statement.

I didn't look at it and said "No Captain, there's nothing I would like to add".

The Captain sat back in his chair. Lefty sat back in his chair. I joined the party by sitting back in my chair.

The Captain looked at Lefty who looked at me. I looked at Lefty then back to the Captain.

"I give up Captain. What is the "else" you're referring to, please?", I said trying to be helpful.

"Did you *sic* that dog on the man up that the street across from the liquor store?", the Captain asked.

I managed not to laugh.

"Whew!", I said letting out a breath. "I thought you were after something more concrete. Something to implicate me in the whole show. Captain Winters, what do you mean by "sic" the dog?"

"Come on, you know what I mean. It's a word or words used to get a dog to attack and kill a person!", the Captain fairly growled.

"Really?", I answered. "That's incredible! I didn't know such a thing was possible. Never heard of anything like that. I never had a dog. I don't even like dogs. However, if you want, I could add that to the statement and the fact I knew nothing about a man, person, thing, or whatever, in or near the street in question. Captain, I was talking to Mr. Schofield when there were three shots, the first went by my ear, the second hit Mr. Schofield, and the third hit him also, but by *that* shot, I was on the floor".

Captain Winters tried to stare me down. Then he raised his voice. "You telling me that that dog just went outside *on his own*, killed that guy and came back in *all on its own*?"

This was all too much for me. I stifled a yawn. "No, I not telling you anything other than what I just wrote down, and that *is,* the damn dog was first on top of the counter, jumped to the floor, bared his fangs at *me* and was about to attack *me* for something I didn't do, an *all* I could do was open the door to let it out or let me out. The dog chose to go outside!"

"Mister James! That's a lot of....", the Captain began but I cut him off.

"Captain, please", I said. "Have you seen that dog? No, you haven't! It's very big, Captain Winters, big enough to do whatever it wants. It went out on it on its own and came back in, *on its own*. That's it!

Before the Captain could answer, the office door burst open and in came Lieutenant Miller.

"Morning, Captain! Lefty!", he said and then noticed me. "Mr. Frigging James, what hell are you doing here?"

"You told me to come in early to make a statement!", I screamed to him getting up and now all four of us were standing.

"Sit down you, you, *Mister* James!", ordered the Captain.

The Lieutenant raised both his hands to the Captain.

"Captain Winters!", he said.

"Don't talk to me and next time KNOCK dammit!", the Captain said.

"Captain, this is my office, remember? I don't knock as a rule and I didn't know you were in here", the Lieutenant said. "I've been looking the Hell all over for you!"

"Well KEEP looking, I got something on this guy and he's going down!"

"SIR!! *Dammit*, there're three feds in your office demanding to see you right *now*, Capitan! Not in a few minutes or a few

HOURS! Right *now*, Sir!!!"

Silence.

"Well…HELL!", Captain said throwing up his arms. Then he was moving to the door but turned to the Lieutenant. "Keep this clown here till I'm through with them bums!".

"Can't do that Capitan", the Lieutenant said shaking his head as was Lefty.

The Captain glared at each of them. "What Hell's wrong with you two? What the Sam-hill do you mean you CAN'T do that?!"

"Can't hold him Capitan, we got *nothing* on him. He's *clean*. I'm the responding officer and the man is *clean*. You read my report. We got to let him go.", the Lieutenant finished.

It got really quiet as we four stood around. The Captain opened his mouth to say something, but then we all could hear Officer Dodd coming down the hall bellowing, "Where's the damn Captain!"

That broke the spell.

"Son-of-a-Bitch!", the Captain spitted out to no one in particular. He pointed his finger at me.

"Don't leave town!!" and slammed the door.

Ridiculous statements don't deserve an answer. I just walked out of the Lieutenants' office, passing him, and Lefty and walked by a scowling Officer Dodd in the hall to my limousine.

I was back in my car, happy to get away from Police La-La Land. It was time to get back to work for the money I was paid and visit Renfro's Grandma.

I dreaded that. She was a dangerous woman and her age didn't make her less so. I had to be careful.

But before I went looking for Ida Mae Louise Jones, called "Grandma Jones" for short, I drove over to Russell Street way and talked to some of my barber-shop friends. They told me that she was still alive. I had not even thought to ask that. They also warned me that she'd gotten, in her old age, even more unpredictable than usual and warned not to "mess with her". But I told them that I had to see her and would come back and give them some juicy gossip later. A few of the customers wished me luck. A few just shook their heads as if saying that no good would come to me where Grandma Jones was concerned. As I was about to leave there, one of the customers asked me if I knew she had moved. I said no and he gave me an address.

Grandma Jones now lived over on the East-Side Way, over the railroad-tracks, on 384 Lily Baxter Street. I had an idea where the street was because I used to try to sell a no-name brand of newspaper on that side of town. But that was 20 years ago but I gave my memory a try and found the street.

I was looking for a house in good shape, since Grandma Jones had money, but most of the houses on that side of town were in good shape, unlike most of on my side.

I was looking left and right when a three-story red-brick house caught my attention. It was on the right-side of the street. I had a feeling about that house, mostly being it was my dream house.

I slowed down and stopped the car in the street to admire the house with its curtained, light-blue accented windows, white-painted three-car garage that looked suspicious and overdone to me. I would never have three cars.

Various flowers were planted and blooming all around a glassed-in front-poach, I could only recognize red-roses, that covered the whole front. A manicured lawn with a blue fence splayed out from the house like a baseball-diamond. Yes, a nice house, my "dream house" and I guessed it cost a fortune, but I could see that it was not the biggest house in the area.

There were a bunch of red-brick houses in the distance, left and right side of the street, that I would have to check out. A car horn blew behind me so I pulled in to the middle-garage way, being careful not to block it.

I sit in my car for a moment, making sure that anyone in the house and any neighbor watching would notice that I was not a thief.

I got out of my car, stretched, closed the car door and walked casually pass the garage to a narrow concrete walk-way that led to the porch steps and the porch-door. I rang the bell. No answer. I rang again. No answer. I knocked twice and still no answer. Against my better judgement I tried and opened the unlocked porch-door, making some noise, and walked up to the front-door, hoping I would be heard. I was about to knock on that door when it was flung open and the longest shotgun I had ever seen was poked in my face.

All I could see in the whole wide world were those two-BIG holes, big as lakes, looking at me. We called them the *"Bad Brothers"*, knowing what chaos they could do at point-blank range. I was still staring at them, my mouth open like a fish, when Grandma Jones, on the other end, started talking.

"Well knock, knock, you're in but WHO the hell are ya!".

"Good afternoon, Grandma Jones….".

"Don't call me Grandma! I ain't your Grandma", ---she said looking me up and down---, "as far as I can tell! Who are you!" She cocked both barrels "I ain't asking again!"

"Yessss Mammm, I am Milton Jones", I said. "I grew up with Hubo. You and I met a long time ago at another house and…"

I didn't get a chance to finish the rest because she turned the shot-gun away from me and un-cocked the barrels.

"Damn right you are child! Why the Hell you didn't say so before! Call me Louise!".

She turned the shot-gun across her chest and tossed it to me. I caught it with both hand across my chest. The damn thing was warm.

She turned and went inside.

"Come on in, damn you, and close the damn door. You letting in a draft and the bastard neighbors might think I got Open House or something", she said with grin looking over her shoulder.

I walked in a large room with the biggest fire-place I'd ever seen. Her furniture was very nice, though a bit dated. A sofa and three stuffed-chairs were covered in plastic. There was a huge dining room-table in the middle of room.

"So, what you want, boy!", she said

The "boy" crap was too much.

"I'm not your boy. And I'm not your Negro!", I replied.

She shook her head side to side. "You whatever I want you to be in MY house, MISTER!"

She pulled a pistol from somewhere and let it hang at her side.

I just looked at her, hefted the shotgun, and matched her smile--- "Lady, did you forget this *damn* ghetto BB-gun you just gave me!", I said.

She laughed and said "That *damn* thing ain't loaded! Do I look stupid!".

Slowly and carefully, while watching her, I opened the breach and looked down to see the damn thing was empty. I froze.

"Mam, please. I didn't come here to fight you. I'm looking for your Grandson Renfro and..."

"What you want with Renfro?", she said in calm voice while swiftly raising and pointed her pistol somewhere below my stomach.

"Nothing bad, I swear to you. I am going the lay this...thing on the floor and tell you why I am looking for him". I bent down and laid the weapon down as gently as a newborn babe and stood up slowly.

She threw the pistol over her head and I cringed as I hear it bounce, waiting for it to go off.

She laughed. "That thing wasn't loaded either".

"Ok, goody!", she said. "Guns are like relatives, they can go off anywhere so you got to be careful, right? Let's drink something. You hungry? Go sit at the table and I'll bring us something", she said.

She walked by me and raised a hand to lovingly rub my face as she went by. I just then realized that she was as tall as me and I'm about six feet.

I sat at the table and could hear her in the kitchen with glasses and plates. It all sounded normal. She came bounding in with a tray with a cake on it and sit it down on the table.

The cake was the strangest thing I'd ever seen, half-chocolate and half-coconut. Magnificent.

She went back in the kitchen and bought out two plates of scrambled-eggs and bacon, then went back again for a bottle of champagne and three glasses. She laid it all out on the table, smiling brightly and humming something that sounded like "Shall we Gather at the River".

She sat and poured the champagne. I didn't hear the typical *pop* when a bottle is opened and saw it was on its half-life.

"Let's *grub!*", she said with that same bright smile that was at once charming and scary. She reached for her glass which was a fruit jar as was mine and we did a toast. "To your underwear!" she said, which was not out of place.

The drink was cold and tasted as it should. She drank all of hers so I followed along. She finished, stood up, and with a fluid motion turned and threw the jar in a corner. It smashed loud, as a fruit-jar should. I did the same with mine and then she laughed and I joined in also. As if on some cue, she sat down and attacked her bacon and eggs as I did but I wondered that they were still warm. Had I been expected?

We finished our bacon and eggs at the same time and she leaned over to me, not smiling, eyes so narrowed that they looked closed.

"Start talking about why you want my Renfro", she said in a croaky voice.

"Do you know where he is?", I said.

"I know where *this* is!", She had pulled another pistol from somewhere.

"Good Lord lady, how many of them things you got around here? Was that one hidden in the cake!"

"Never mind *where* I got it from, mind that this one's loaded, buddy-boy!", she said.

The condemned man ate a hearty meal I thought and gave up. Client privacy or not, I was not going to get plugged.

"Ok, ok", I said with a sigh and sat back in my chair.

"Yesterday a guy named "Jones" hired me to find Renfro and give him a message. The guy wants the Forty-thousand back that he says Renfro took from him. He also mentioned three girls were also taken but he did not want them back".

Grandma frowned at that.

"He gave me a week to find Renfro and there would be a meet, within two days, where Renfro must bring back the dough", I said

"His name can't be *Jones*. What's his real name?", she said.

"I don't know, I thought the name he gave was bogus from the go", I said.

"Describe him!"

"Well, about five-foot 8, low cut hair, big-head, brown eyes that seem too close together, and he smelled like, like…", I said.

"Like cheap perfume?", she interrupted.

"Well, yes. He wore a black suit with a black-stick pin topped with a little white pearl at the bottom of his tie. The pin was up-side-down".

"Yeah, it's him, the Bastard", she said more to herself. She got up from the table and laid the gun down on a counter.

"That one was really loaded", she said.

"I believe you", I said and she smiled and went through the living-room. I could see where she stopped at the bottom of some stairs in another room.

"Renfro", she called. "RENFRO!", she called up again. "Get down here!".

By then I had got up and stood next to her. There was a silence then I heard a door close and someone walking toward the steps.

Louise looked at me. "You packing, son?"

"You kidding? No Mam", I said opening my coat. She patted me down, enjoying every minute of it. I was glad I left my gun in the car.

I heard someone coming down the stairs and we both looked up to see Mr. Renfro Jones make his grand appearance.

I had not seen him in fifteen years. He had changed from a skinny tall guy to fat tall guy but looking closer, as he got to the bottom of the stairs and loomed over me, fat was not the right word.

There was no fat, just muscle. Skinny Renfro had turned into a six-foot-four monster Renfro. He eyed us both with no fear with a silly kind of quirky half-smile that smelled of…aloofness and arrogance that grated on my nerves. I despise arrogance. My reaction was automatic. I stepped toward him, trying to close the short distance between us, ready to take a swing at him.

Grandma grabbed my arm and stopped me.

"No!", she said. "He's always like that. It doesn't mean nothing".

Renfro didn't like that. His smile vanished and we eyed each until Louise had enough of our macho silliness.

"Say *Hello* to our damn guest, Ren. Where's your God-Damn manners, boy!".

Renfro looked at her and she looked back as if she was about to jump him. He eyed me.

"*Hello,* Mister James! What drags you over this way?", he said.

"*You,* Mister Jones, and it's strictly business. I have a message for you, that's all".

Louise chimed in, "Wonderful. Let's all saunter and kip to the dining room. You both go and wait as I make damn bastard addict coffee".

Renfro kept his eyes on me and said "I don't want no coffee".

"I did'nt ASK if you wanted coffee, did I? Now go sit the Hell down and wait!", she said.

We men did what she ordered all the while watching each other, of which I got tired of and quit playing. Funny, I thought, the man was taller and at least 80 pounds heavier but was he afraid of me? A little voice in my head said "No".

We sat and I cut myself a piece of cake from the coconut side. Renfro cut from the chocolate side and I could smell how good it was all the way across the table. I sat back and waited for the coffee and Louise came in with a tray, pot, and three cups, red, white, and blue. I appreciated her sense of humor but Renfro didn't seem to notice. She set the tray down, gave out the cups and poured. She overfilled Renfro's and sat and sipped and we did likewise.

As we set our cups down, I started talking.

"Renfro, yesterday a guy names Jones came to me with a job. He wanted me to find you and give you a message", I said and just for the hell of it I forked and ate piece of cake. It was really good.

"Jones?", he said. "What the Bastard look like?".

"I already told Miss Louise and I ain't saying it again. It's the same "Bastard" both of you know", I said looking to Louise.

"Yeah", she said. "It's the same pimp-ass no good SOB bastard Jody "JJ" Jones. HE ain't related to us at all! Let's get that straight now, Mr. De-tective!", she said.

"He told me he was, Grandma", Renfro said.

"He's a liar, back and front!", she said.

Well, at least I had the full name of my client.

"Here's the message, Renfro. Mr. JJ Jones demands the $40,000, he says *you* stole from him, back by…Saturday. He says you can keep the three girls, do what you want with them or even adapt them if you want to", I said.

Renfro chuckled, "Adapt them…"

How he come up with Saturday?", Renfro asked, looking down.

"That was part of the work. He gave me a week to find you, so after I'm finished here, I'll go back to my office and I bet you he'll show up, cause the place is for sure being watched, so I'll tell him I found you and gave you the message. Since today is Wednesday, two days from now is what I call Saturday. Anyway, one damn day won't harm nothing, all is wants is a meeting time and place so you can give him back his money", I said.

No one said anything. Then Renfro looked up.

"I-did-not-take his money! All I took was my share, a share that he owed me. So ain't no money to hand over", Renfro said.

"That, Brother Renfo. is between you and Mr. JJ", I said. "I won't even be in sight. He also told me to tell you that if you don't give the money back, he's going to send his boys to "un-arrange" you".

Louise jumped in. "What the heck is "un-arrange?"".

"Well, he said Renfro would know what that meant. Care to tell us?", I said.

Renfro looked down, right and then left. He sighed and said "Means they just come to kill me and cut me up into little pieces. The cut in pieces part has never been done before, but I wouldn't put it pass him".

"Ok,", I said. "Mr. JJ wants you to pick a neutral place. So, where do you want to meet with him, please? I thought it was time to be friendly so I could just get the Hell out of there.

"I got no reason to meet him, James. I don't own him any money. I don't want to see him. Tell him he can go to…"

Louise interrupted him.

"Tell him we meet here in this house!".

"Mama!!", Renfro objected.

"I'm not your Mama! I'm your *Grand-Mother* and don't forget that!", she said.

"Ok Grand-Mother, but please, not here. It's too dangerous! You could get hurt!", Renfro said.

Then I had a horrible thought and said so.

"Hey, does this JJ guy know where you live Miss Louise?", I said.

Renfro caught that. "Oh, crap!! Do you think you were followed here? They could be right outside this minute!". He started to rise.

"Not hardly, I didn't see a tail the whole time I been working on this. But that's not the point. Does Mr. JJ Jones know where you live"?

"No", came the answer from Louise and Renfro in unison.

"I moved here three months ago. Some friends of mine are putting on a good show that I still live at the old house. I own both houses. No way whats-his-name could know where I am", Louise said.

I said, "Good. That's a relief! Ok, I'll go on back to my office and wait for Mr. Jones, no relation. You got a phone here?"

"Yep", Louise said and wrote it down.

I got up to leave and then got curious.

"I'm curious", I said. "Just between us, what's with the "keep the three girls" thing?"

Renfro said nothing.

Louise said "Damn prostitution!"

"Grandma, please".

"Grandma please my ass! Didn't I tell you NOT to get in that business! Didn't I beg you NEVER to get in that damn business!", she said screaming.

Renfro sank in his chair as far as he could. "I'm sorry Grandma".

"Sorry AIN'T SHIT! You hear me! "SORRY AIN'T EVEN CLOSE! "Damn! You so-called *Men!* You all ain't worth nothing!" she said

"I'm sorry…", Renfro said.

"Where them three girls at! You didn't tell me about em!".

"I sent them back to their homes. All three were run-aways. I gave them a thousand each and sent them home, Grandma. I was no good at that business. It was all JJ's idea, we started last year, and from day one I wanted out. About a month ago, when I moved in with you here, I took my share that JJ was holding and took off with the girls also. He let me go, Grandma", Renfro said.

"Why just them three! You got some kind of fantasy or something!!", Louise said.

Renfro just shook his head.

"Why them DAMN THREE", Renfro!", Louise screamed.

"They were under-aged, Grandma. The oldest was maybe 15. They should have been in school or something, not doing what…"

"Well, Mister Robin Hood, that just sounds half-ass good! How many more "girls" are we talking about!".

Renfro thought. "Could be fifteen or twenty more, now. I don't know."

Grandma thought. "Don't sound like a big operation…he'd have to, to work them hard to make the kind of money you talking about".

She looked at Renfro. "WAS he working them hard---, *Mister* Renfro!"

"Yes, Mam".

"How long?"

"What?"

"The business! How *long*, damn you!"

"Well, like it said, but it's got to be over a year now".

"A whole year…. all day, every day?", asked Louise

"As far as I know, Yes Mam".

"Don't call me Mam", Louise said getting from the table going to the counter.

"I couldn't stand being there every day, Grandma, no way I could be there and watch what was going on every day, every night! Now JJ, oh he loved it. He would be there all the time, *managing*, he called it".

Grandma was only half listening. She had the pistol in her hand now, the one that was loaded. I watched her warily. Renfro turned to watch her.

"Mr. James", she said.

"Yes, Mam?", I answered.

"I depend on you to bring that punkass no snookie dumShit here to meet Renfro. You call and tell us the exact time him and his "boys" are coming", she said while pointing the gun at Renfro's head who calmly watched her.

"I'll do that, Mam", I said. "You can depend on me. Err, just wanted to remind you that there was no talk of his "boys" being involved in the meet".

She lowered the gun to her side. Renfro turned to look at me with no expression at.

"It doesn't matter what the Hell he *said*. A Son of a Snake is always a liar! He will come with them, money or no money, being the coward, he is. Set it up and damn make sure your ass ain't here. Understand?", she said.

"I understand, Miss Louise, but I get the feeling that JJ will not give me a choice and will just strong-arm me here. If so…", I said

"If so", Renfro said with a grin that was out of place, "That would be too-bad for you Brother James, but…we'll just play it by ear. You say that damn Mr. Jody Jones we meet in this house, this coming Saturday at 3:00pm sharp. If he comes early the deal is off. If he comes late, the deal is off. In any case he can go to *Hell* before Saturday and save us all a lot of trouble."

He turned his smile to his Grand-Mother who smiled back at him. Neither said a thing. I didn't dare say anything. I just wanted to get the heck out of there so I got up and left.

It was still Private Eye early, about 10:00pm, when I parked my rig in our building's parking lot. I locked her up to make sure she didn't move around the lot as she sometimes did, walked in the building, and up my side entrance stairway that nobody was supposed to use but everybody did. I saw that my office-door was open, unlocked. Before I could come in there came a voice from inside.

"Come on in pal, what took you so long?"

I came in.

Mr. Jody *JJ* Jones had come calling, sitting at my desk with his shoes on top of same. I glared at him. He raised a glass of whiskey at me, making a toast.

"Man", he said, "Kinda unhealthy of you leaving this whiskey un-capped all this time. I hope it's still good", he said as he sipped.

"Take your damn dirty shoes off my desk AND got out of my chair! I said".

He just sat there and glared back, but the smile had left his cheeks like a blown out cheap candle.

"Oh, ain't we touchy today. You carrying a gun now, pal? Is that why you so brave?".

"I'm not your pal! I'm brave when I have to be and how the Hell did get in here? The place was locked!", raising my voice higher.

"Ok, then we ain't pals, but *friend*, I don't answer dumb questions".

He took his legs of my desk and the shoes came with them. He stood up and walked slowly around my desk to the customer's chair, waved me grandly to desk, waited for me to sit and then he sat down.

"Now", he said. "Ain't this just marvelous?"

"Ain't, ain't a word and I don't see what's *marvelous* about this whole deal!", I said as I reached for the undisturbed glass of whiskey.

"Ain't" IS a beautiful word Mister and not you anybody else in this *world* can stop me from using it! Now, stop stalling and tell me if you found Renfro!"

"YEAH! I found Mister Renfro Jones! It was not that hard to do. Makes me wonder about your game, Mr. Jones."

"That's as nice as a bunch of cute little sheep, but I ain't playing no game. You find him or not!"

"I found him, but first let's talk cash. I owe you some money back and…".

"Get real, *pal*. I don't want no scratch back. If you found him, I'm happy even if I don't talk happy. You keep it all, maybe I need you for another job in my next lifetime or something, heh?", Mr. JJ Jones said.

"Ok. I have a message from him to you", I said, sipping the last of my dusty whiskey that warm as a crow's feet.

"Well give it up man, it's getting late. I got a bank to rob tonight", he said with a smile.

"Mister Renfro says the money he took was his share of what you owed him from the business, whatever that was. You don't get no money back".

"I don't like THAT at all", he said.

"Next, the three girls he doesn't have no more. He sent them packing with some of his loot, so that subject is *none of your damn business*. That's from Mister Renfro, not me", I lied.

Mister JJ moved to edge of the chair.

"I don't give spit about him and his woman-loving-self, or them three girls, or *you* as far as that goes! Did he name our *business*, Mister James?"

"Thank God he didn't and I made sure NOT ask him. I didn't need to know that", I lied again.

"Now that's good to hear, you looking out for my interests. Wonderful! Now, where is he?"

"Grandma Jones' place", I said.

"Hell he is! We been watching that house two months. Every now and then she has a visitor, every now and then she goes shopping is what they tell me. Renfro ain't there. What you trying to pull?", he raved.

"You really don't where Grandma Jones is, do you?", I said grinning. "You didn't get one of your goons to follow me around?"

"Why the hell should I do that? The name of the *game* is

Renfro, I wanted him found, that's why I hired your tired ass, remember? I was just covering all the bases with Grandma Jones' house. Anything else you want to know!"

"Ok, good", I said. "That's really good"

"You said that already so give before I plug you where you sit, then we both lose!", he said reaching inside his coat.

"Only he who is shot is the real loser, Mr. Jones", I said. "Ok, Grandma Jones must have moved him, he's at 438 Lily Baxter Street on the East Side", I said.

Mr. JJ sat back in his chair, took his hand out of his coat, his face a look of disbelief, mistrust, but all in all I think he just did not believe what he was hearing.

"Straight-up?", he asked.

"Straight-up. That's where he is now, you all been watching the wrong house", I replied.

"We watching that joint for two months and he gets clean away somewhere else! You sure about that address, pal, you ain't pulling down my lids, are you?".

"I'm not pulling down nothing Mr. Jones. I just left him. Renfro says to meet him at that address at 3:00pm this coming Saturday. He says to come alone. He says that if you early the deal is off. If you come late the deal is off".

"Hell, it is. Deal's never off, Brother. That seems to be good time to have a meeting, it doesn't block nothing I had planned, Mr. JJ Jones said".

"I hope so, Mr. Jones, if that's your real name. Also, tonight concludes our business please. I am closed. I got a hot bath waiting for me and it's getting colder by the minute".

Mr. Jones just sat there in that chair, so relaxed he seemed to sink in it.

Then he stood up. I stood up.

"If this is all wrong, Mr. James, I'll be coming back to see you", Mr. Jones said.

"I'll be waiting but you got what you paid for", I said.

"I'd better", he said, and Mr. Jody JJ Jones got up and walked out of office without so much as a damn Thank-You.

The rest of week was uneventful. Then came Saturday night around 9:00 o'clock.

I'm in my living room curled up in a blanket on my couch with myself and the rest of "Nikki's", slurping away, watching a western on the TV with the sound off. I love westerns. But my happy time was shattered by the "BAM BAM" that fists made on my front door. My whole body jumped straight up in the air.

I came down and got up with "Damn! Damn!", to another BAM! BAM!, on my lips, but worse in my head and staggered to the door. Not thinking I opened it, which was not very smart because I was not so beloved these days in this town. There could have been a guy with gun ready to knock me off.

Luck was with me because there stood Detective Lieutenant Harvey Miller in all his stately glory with what looked like a new suit with all the trimmings.

"Lieutenant Miller!", I said with my best "I'll be damned" voice. Then I burped loudly and almost did something else.

"You going to a funeral or something? If you did you missed a turn somewhere. Nothing but the living in here, Buddy", I said.

He was not impressed and just pushed pass me saying "I need

to talk to you".

"Well, that's obviously", I said. "Come on in why the Hell don't you!", I said closing the door and letting out an even louder burp.

"I'm *in*, Mister James. You alone?", he asked looking around.

"Depends on what you got in mind!", laughing at my own joke.

"I got in mind to *tell* you something", he said and pointed a finger up and down to the ceiling to signal if there was someone upstairs. I nodded yes and he pointed to the kitchen and I had move fast to catch up with him. The kitchen-table was waiting patiently, so we sat down.

"So, what's going on", I asked

"*You*, are what's going on, Mister James", he said and started to count on his fingers as I watched.

"I got, one, two, three, four, five, six, seven, eight…no wait, I got seven dead guys and one wounded on my hands and I think you got *everything* to do with it!".

"*Me?* Why me? I don't know what you talking about. Why blame me?", I asked.

"Well, because your name seems to come up where ever these bodies *pop-up*!"

"Well back to ya, whatever it is I had nothing to do with it. I been here all day!".

"Have you?".
"Yeah, Harvey. Come on, give me a break. What's happened?", I asked.
He told me and it went like this-----

Saturday 3:00pm sharp at Grandma Jones' house.

A car pulls up in front and six guys get out, pistols and shot-guns in full view and rush the house.

They're close to house, in full stride, when a shot-gun and a pistol open fire from an open, second floor middle-window. Two men go down, but still manage to get off a few shots with pistols of various calibers and shotgun blasts. The other four guys stop and shoot up at the open window also, pistols in *each* hand.

Shots are traded and there's an audible grunt from the window. The grunt seemed to encourage the men to storm the house, so they go through the porch-door and the front-door, both doors being suspiciously wide-open, and are surprised by a standing and braced Grandma Jones with a black-stock Tommy-Gun. She laughs and opens fire and two more guys go down, shot to pieces.

The other two guys had jumped to either side of the front-door and both stick their hand-guns around the corners to blast away, trying to hit Grandma which they actually do because she's hit once, but they don't know it. They both shoot their guns empty, both hands, then drop them, pull out two fresh ones, each. There were a lot of guns in play that day.

Quiet. The two men peep around the corner and no Grandma, so they rush in. Just then a wounded guy, shoot twice, comes running down the stairs with a gun in each hand. He gets to bottom of the stairs and not hesitating comes around the corner blasting away at the two guys who return fire. Then Grandma Jones, her left-side blooded, comes out of another room and opens up again with her reloaded

Tommy-Gun, blasting away. Bullets are flying everywhere, but a lot of them were wild, missing targets. The two guys, one of which being JJ Jones, were also blasting away.

A man who went berserking down the stairs, who was hit at least six times, empties both his pistols, missing both men. He then reached somewhere and threw something that landed between the two guys who are shot-up but still shooting. These two men looked down at what was thrown, just as Grandma shots more bullets in them as she goes down shot another two times. Looks like she was hit in the cross-fire between the man from the stairs and the other two men.

Then there was an explosion from the grenade that this Renfro character threw and fell down dead as a loon. The explosion set the house on fire, however, at the first shots the neighbors had called the Police. At least one neighbor tried to call the National Guard who thankfully did not answer.

Grandma Jones somehow managed to crawl out the back door and propped herself against a tree. She was unconscious when they found her and taken to the hospital. About 4:00am this morning after surgery she was eager to talk and we took her statement. It went like this….

"I talked for a long time with Renfro last week. He told me it all had nothing to do with money or girls. Mister JJ Jones gave him the money because Renfro wanted out of the business and demanded his cash back. Renfro also asked for the three girls because they were under-age. He told JJ, "I can use them, Man", and JJ being the dumb-ass he was, was suspicious and believed Renfro was starting a special kind of "service", something that maybe could put JJ out of business. When JJ asked for a bogus meet to get his money back, Renfro knew that he would come with his boys to just kill him. What? Are we related to JJ? Hell no! JJ was a damn Harris and always wanted to be in the Jones family so he just changed his name, silly man.

Where did we get the grenade? My dead-to-damn-early Husband…Bless his sweet ass, had it in the basement. I thought it was a dud, Renfro wanted to try it. What? Well, like I say, we both decided that JJ was coming to kill anybody in house so we got drunk they night before and planned what to do, but I tell ya, to die was NOT part of the plan. Renfro thought the bastard had only three guys and himself but six came.

Renfro was upstairs with a shot-gun in one hand and a pistol in the other. He caught em by surprise! HA! They thought we both were upstairs. It was his idea. He was a good boy, Renfro. Just got mixed up with wrong damn crowd...like I did...What! The Tommy-Gun? Hell, it's was made special for me and its mine and you can't have it. Illegal? Like hell it is! When I get out of here, I want it back or some bastard is in big trouble!! Leave me alone now, I'm tired...."

Silence at my house.

"I knew somebody was gonna buy it, but not like that", I said finally.

"You should have let me know what you were doing. Maybe I could have done something", Harvey said.

"No, I didn't think it would get that crazy", I said getting up from the table. "Come on".

We went back to living-room. It was my attempt to get Harvey up and gone from my house.

"Thanks for coming by and telling me, Harv".

"No problem...hey! Don't call me "Harv!."
"Ok. So, don't you call me "Mil", I said facing him.
He stepped toward me. "I never, ever, called you *Mil!*, he shouted.

"Yes, you did! A couple of times", I said raising my voice sing-song. We were face-to-face.

"You know", Harvey said sticking a finger in my chest, "I got all these dead guys on my hands and here you stand there without a scratch. How you manage that? Just luck?".

"Well, yeah. I guess so", I said.

"If that's the case, Brother you need to go down to the casino, you'd break the bank!", Harvey said.

"Oh, NO! I ain't no good at that crap! Are you nuts", I said getting riled.

Harvey opened his mouth to say something, shut it, then turned from me, sniffing around. I rolled my eyes.

"Hey...err, what the *Hell* is that smell?", he said.

"What smell?", I said lying like Hell. "I don't smell nothing! You losing it or what?"

Harvey was sniffing around the couch and then upwards in the air when a sultry, enchanting, voice from the stairs said "Up-here-boys".

We both looked up to see JennieLee, wearing see-through, full-body black tights with a white

lightning-bolt symbol sewed in from the top of her neck to the nether regions, looking down on us with those yellow-green eyes. I knew to avoid those eyes. Whatever else was seen didn't count for nothing. The eyes had it.

Harvey didn't know about the eye thing. He got the full blast. She locked down on him and rocked his world. I shook my head for her to let him go. To my surprise she did. From Harvey came a small "hmmm", as if to object.

"Good evening", she said looking at Harvey. "The smell? Well, it's something we women can turn off and turn on whenever we want to. Just forget it, Mr. Policeman. No one gonna believe you any way", JennieLee said.

"How's Grandma doing?", I said loudly trying to get Harvey's attention. It worked.

"Who?", he said turning to me, a deep frown objecting to be interrupted from enjoying whatever he was enjoying. "Oh, she died 5:00am this morning. She had a smile on her face. Doctors can't figure out why", Harvey said then looking back up at JennieLee.

"Let em keep figuring", I said. "They good at that. Damn, what a business I'm in. Makes me think about being a Copper again, something simple and...."

Harvey looked back at me.

"Sorry bud! No vacancies! Not with US! Why don't you go back to them silly, arrogant, no-good government boys and... aaaaah, *that*, by the way reminds me of something. The Captain asks that you come see him tomorrow".

"*Ask*s", I said. "He's never *asked* me to do anything. He simply orders. What's wrong with him?"

"Well, Mr. James, it seems that at least three federal boys from three agencies want to talk to you *bad*. They ordered our illustrious Captain to produce you by 8:00 am tomorrow or *his* big-but is in *big* trouble", Harvey said with satisfaction.

"That early, 8:00am! I can't do it Harv", I said looking upstairs.

Harvey looked to the stairs also, where JennieLee was still watching.

"Officer, please. There's no way he can be there *that* early. I forbid it. Could you please make some arrangements to cover for him?", JennieLee cooed.

Silence.

"You bet", came the reply from Harvey, reluctantly breaking his gaze from her. He looked to me with a scowl, as if to say why was I there. I had my old Harvey back.

"Don't call me *Harv*! I'll let you in on something, *Mil,* and you didn't get it from me. That guy in liquor store caper…"

"What about him? That was no caper, what are talking about?"

"Turns out that not a single one of his identifications match him at all: name, birth certificate, Army Service Number, Social Security Number, or even blood-type, all belonged to a guy that died in 1948. The government boys think he's some kind of deep-cover spy. Of course, their very astute, and intelligent conclusion is that *you* might *know* something about him!", Harvey said bending over to slap his knee with a big laugh.

"That's brilliant, just brilliant!", I said. "I get lost in a part of town I never been in, I'm being followed, I duck in the *only* place open, the owner gets shoot and they think I *know* something! Fantastic! But what do you mean by *spy*? What kind of spy?".

"Of course, the worse kind James. The *Soviet* kind!", Harvey said, now laughing like a crazy man as he walked toward the door. He stopped to take a last look at JennieLee, but she was not there. He stopped laughing.

He looked at me and laughed anew, all the way to the door and out. I could hear his laughter as he walked to his car, got in and slammed the door. The car started and tires squealed, like something wild going its own way.

The whole time I stood there frozen in front of my couch. Then something about Harvey's laughter made me remember something. I looked to my stairs. My mind saw JennieLee's silhouette burned in the wall.

I smiled thankfully and went upstairs.

The End